Rusty Wilson's

....

Bigfoot Campfire Stories

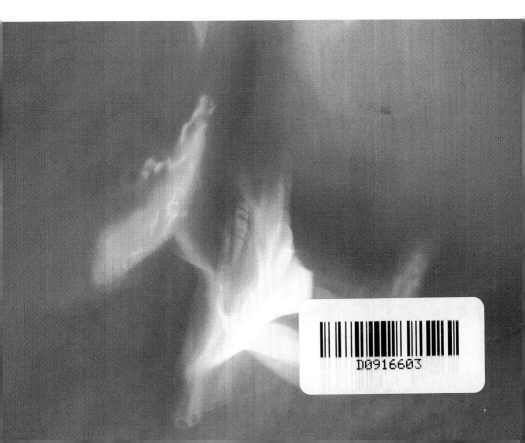

I've spent a lot of my life sitting around a campfire, swapping stories with my fishing clients. We always have fun, but sometimes we don't sleep too well afterwards.
—*Rusty Wilson*

· F O R ·

Jeannette
truth seeker

Contents

Foreword

· ·

by Rusty Wilson

Greetings fellow adventurers.

How do I know you're an adventurer? Anyone that likes Bigfoot stories has to like adventure—and mystery. I'm a big fan of both, and I know you'll really enjoy these stories.

I've spent a lot of my life sitting around a campfire, swapping stories with my fishing clients. We always have fun, but sometimes we don't sleep too well afterwards.

I've been collecting Bigfoot stories for years. This book represents the best of the lot, and believe me, there's been a lot.

So, pull up a chair or log, kick back with some hot chocolate, and be prepared to read some tales that will make your hair stand on end, or maybe make you wonder if you might like to meet the Big Guy himself.

(Please note that the names of the people and some locations have been changed, in case you get the itch to go Bigfooting.)

[1] Terror on the River

This first story in this collection was told to me by my good friend Craig, an ex-river rat and fellow flyfishing guide. We were sitting around a campfire high up on Grand Mesa, near Grand Junction, Colorado, one late July evening after a great day of lake fishing.

Craig told his story with such conviction that I was scared to go to bed that night. Grand Mesa has been the site of several Bigfoot sightings and is perfect Bigfoot habitat, with its many lakes and large expanses of untrod forests. Of course, I didn't have the heart to tell Craig this.

I was a raft guide at the time, working what's called the Daily out of Moab, Utah, a very popular run on the Colorado River. It's tourist intensive, and I was feeling burned out and had two weeks off, so I decided to solo canoe the Green, one of my favorite things to do.

The Green River has a long stretch between the town of Green River, Utah and where it meets the Colorado at the Confluence. This is a very mellow run and popular with canoeists because there are no rapids. It's made of two lengths called Labyrinth and Stillwater Canyons.

It can take a good week to 10 days to run both (about 120 miles), and I made arrangements with a jetboat company to pick me up on day 10 at the Confluence, which is standard operating procedure. You can't canoe below the Confluence because of the rapids in Cataract Canyon.

A friend dropped me and my canoe off, and I put in early in the morning at the Green River Geyser, a few miles out of town. I immediately felt the sense of peace that always comes to me when solo canoeing in big desert canyons. The river was slow and mellow and I could immediately feel all my tensions melting away.

That first day, I saw only a couple of other boats, both being small non-commercial rafts. I spent the night on a large sandbar that I'd camped on before. I watched a spectacular sunset and played my Peruvian flute into the evening.

The next day, I was just dilly-dallying, drinking coffee and lazing around camp, hanging out on the beach. As I was finally getting ready to take off, a small raft with two people came drifting along, and they stopped, pulling the raft up onto the beach. They seemed disturbed and asked me if I'd heard the weird noises the previous night. They had apparently camped about two miles above me.

I told them I hadn't, and they said some large animal had been up on the rim screaming at them. It didn't sound like a mountain lion and had really scared them, so much so that they were now going to take out early at Mineral Bottom instead of going all the way to the Confluence.

Mineral Bottom is where Labyrinth Canyon ends and Stillwater begins, but they were still a good two to three days away from it.

This animal had screamed at them most of the night, they told me, and sounded very big and angry. They expressed concern for my traveling solo, offering to let me tag along with them. In fact, they almost begged me to tag along, and I felt their concerns were genuine, but I shrugged the whole affair off as being a mountain lion and forgot about it not long after they were gone.

There's not much out in the canyons that scares me, I've spent my entire life in that country and know its flora and fauna like the back of my hand. I've hiked it, dirt biked it, flown over it, and jeeped it.

I had a wonderful day, and slept well on the beach that night, entranced by the desert stars. The Green was my second home, and I loved being out there.

The third day went well until mid to late afternoon, when I noticed that the river was rising. I paid attention, but didn't worry. It must be raining somewhere upstream, it could be miles and miles away. But by evening, I was having trouble locating a good place to camp, as the river had risen enough that the beaches were being inundated.

Now it was getting late and I was becoming a bit worried. The river had risen enough that everything looked different. I couldn't find the camp spot I wanted, one I'd camped at on another trip.

I kept floating and looking, and by the time it was almost dark I decided to boat over into a cottonwood grove that was partially underwater and tie up to one of the trees.

I left lots of rope length in case the river kept rising so I wouldn't get in trouble and be pulled under, ate a quick cold dinner, and tried to create a makeshift bed in the canoe, which was pretty difficult. But the water soon lulled me to sleep, as I was really tired. I'd been on the river all day with no real breaks.

This was my third day on the river, and I knew I was getting close to Mineral Bottom, as the river had been running high and fast and it typically takes about four or five days to get there. Mineral Bottom has a place for take-outs and an access road (such that it is—dropping off the Island in the Sky and a bit hairy).

I don't know what time it was when I woke up, my senses heightened by the rising river. I checked the rope with my flashlight. All was well, the river seemed to have stopped rising.

I had just drifted back to sleep, somewhat uncomfortable, when I heard something whoosh in the river not far from my canoe. It was odd, it sounded like a large rock dropping into the water.

I thought about it and listened for awhile, then decided it was a beaver slapping its tail. Beavers are nocturnal, but it didn't occur to me until later that a beaver probably wouldn't be out on the river in such high waters, as beaver tend to stay near the smaller estuaries where they have their dams.

I drifted off and again woke to the sound, only closer. That was followed by another, and then a large rock that landed in the water close enough that it sprayed me. I was being barraged by someone.

I turned on my flashlight and shone it around, seeing no one. I then pulled my watch from my pack. It was five a.m.

At that point, what must have been a huge rock nicked the side of my canoe, causing it to tip a bit, and I could even hear a little wood splintering. Whoever had thrown the rock had possibly seen my light and my location.

I was now both scared and mad, and I started yelling and cussing at whoever was doing this to cut it out. This was followed by a pause and then another rock thrown close to the canoe. These rocks seemed like they were very large from the splashes they made.

I now figured I had two choices: stay put and get maimed, killed, or sunk by a rock, or get away. I fumbled with the rope, afraid to use the flashlight to see what I was doing, and eventually got the canoe free as more rocks came in.

I pulled out into the current in the dark and immediately heard a sound from the rim high above, a sound I will never forget, one I've never heard before or since.

It started out as a very loud and deep growling and soon turned into a high pitched undulating scream, echoing through the canyon.

I've never heard anything so loud and massive, it had to come from a very large creature. It was so powerful it had an almost electrical component to it, with multiple frequencies. It made my blood run cold and scared me almost to death.

The rim was probably a good 1,000 feet above me, so I felt I would be safe out on the river, and I started trying to read the currents in the early dawn, an impossible task. The river had risen enough that I wasn't afraid as much of running into a sandbar as being run over by a large log or branch, but I managed to stay afloat as dawn gradually made my surroundings visible.

The river had gone down some. I stayed out in the middle, away from the rim where the weird stuff had happened, to my right.

As the day became lighter and things more visible, I could make out someone running on the rim, keeping up with me, though high above and some distance away. Whoever or whatever it was, was very fast.

This really scared me, that someone would do this, but I knew they had no chance of coming off that rim, it was just too sheer and high. They were so high up I could just barely make out a figure on the skyline.

It's hard to express what I was feeling as it became late morning, and by now this had been going on for several hours, the figure following along on the rim.

It now occurred to me that there are places where one can come down off the rim, and I was in a heightened state of fear and flight, a sustained adrenalin flow that was making me more tense and nearly physically sick by the moment.

I hadn't eaten anything since the light dinner the evening before, and I knew I couldn't keep anything down anyway. I was also in a state of disbelief, the Green had always been my sanctuary and refuge.

I was beginning to think I was going mad, except I kept thinking of the rafters who had stopped and of their report. Whatever this thing was, it had incredible endurance and speed to keep up with me like it was, as I estimated I was moving a good six or seven m.p.h. on the river.

By now I was rowing as fast as possible, just focusing on getting to Mineral Bottom. I knew I was almost to Bowknot Bend, and it would be about a mile from the takeout once I exited the loop. I entered the meander and looked up, but there was nothing on the rim. It must have given up.

But soon, to my horror, I noticed a large manlike creature, all dark brown, swimming in the current behind me and to my right, and I watched in disbelief as it slowly gained on me.

It must have been huge and very powerful to make headway like that, as I was in the direct river current, which was relatively swift from yesterday's storm. I was beginning to think I was hallucinating.

I rowed even harder, scared beyond words. I could make out its arms, which seemed to be very long and powerful, and its head was huge. Its shoulders were massive and very muscular as they pulled it through the water.

What I could see was totally covered with dark hair or fur, except for around its facial features, where there appeared to be lighter skin. I couldn't really see it that well through the water being flung up by its powerful strokes, but it reminded me of a cross between a giant ape and a human. It was totally unreal.

Soon I was at Mineral Bottom, and I've never felt such a sense of relief. The creature was still behind me, but as

I rowed to the banks of the river, hoping and praying that someone was there, it seemed to fall back. If no one was there, I had no idea what would happen.

My prayers were answered as I jumped out of the canoe and saw a raft group putting in to do Stillwater. I could barely talk, but asked if I could get a ride out with the driver, as I was sick, and they said that would be fine. I was shaking and felt like I would pass out, but managed to keep it together.

I wanted to tell them not to get into the water, but I decided with that many people, they would be OK, and I knew they would think I was crazy, so I didn't say anything.

We loaded my canoe onto their trailer, but I didn't even care what happened to it, I knew I would never use it again. In fact, I ended up giving it to a friend. I wanted nothing to do with it.

He was incredulous when I told him the story, but I told him I was moving away and would never use it again, and he seemed to accept that.

I haven't been on a river since, and I quit my job and moved to Colorado, where I work as a carpenter. I will never go into the canyons again. I feel like I've lost a very important part of my life, but it's just how it is. I've seen several therapists, and none understand, but they all tell me I have symptoms of PTSD.

Not long after this, against my advice, my friend went down Labyrinth in my canoe. I literally begged him not to and regretted giving it to him.

He woke up one morning to find the canoe missing, even though he'd carefully tied it off. He had to hitch a ride with some rafters, and they found the canoe a few miles downstream on a beach, smashed to smithereens. This was a valuable craft, a genuine handmade red-cedar canoe from Maine, and no one in their right mind would have destroyed it. My friend said he found several huge human-like footprints next to the boat in the sand.

I know exactly what did the damage, and I also know it probably was capable of doing it with its bare hands. Why it didn't harm my friend I don't know, maybe it was just angry at people in general.

I never saw the creature again, though I heard its scream many times in my nightmares.

[2] A Most Unusual Rescue

. . . .

This story came my way while sitting around a campfire near Hahns Peak, Colorado, where I'd been guiding several guys on a flyfishing trip. Johnny was a really nice guy, quiet and soft-spoken, and I wonder if that didn't maybe have something to do with his rescue in the story he told us.

Seems the Big Fellow took a liking to him. I'm glad he did, because otherwise I would never have had the pleasure of watching Johnny catch a six-pound rainbow trout.

My name is Johnny, and I own a ski shop in a small mountain town in the San Juan Mountains of Colorado. I like to be outdoors, and I particularly like to climb mountains. Used to, anyway, before I wrecked my knees climbing and skiing—and had a huge paradigm shift. Let me explain what I mean by that.

One day, I set out to climb Redcloud Peak (14,034 feet), in the San Juan Mountains. It was late summer, the deadly monsoon season. The San Juans are full of iron ore and attract lightning like no other mountains in Colorado, and the monsoons of late summer bring perfect lightning conditions.

Getting an early start, I headed out from the tiny town of Lake City. I'd been told that the Redcloud trailhead was on the road to Cinnamon Pass, which I'd never been on, though later I would have a number of adventures there.

Having grown up in Colorado, to me a mountain pass is simply any road that goes over a mountain. So, I left Lake City and took the first road that looked like it went over a mountain, not realizing that I'd inadvertently taken the wrong fork in the road.

I'm not the bravest of high-altitude drivers, and it still amazes me that I did this, just took off upwards and onwards. I could see a single track going up a very steep mountain, but I couldn't see where it actually went.

After climbing a few hundred feet, I was soon at a scree field, the road now just a faint flatness across what looked like a 45-degree slope of very loose rock, and I could now see that it ended high above at an old abandoned mine.

The rocks were beginning to settle under my Jeep, and since there was no place to turn around, I slowly, very slowly, backed down the road, narrow and steep, hoping I could stay on track.

That should have been my first sign that maybe it was a good day to go home and read a book or go shopping, or whatever people do who don't go adventuring outdoors. When I got back down, I rechecked my map. It had led me astray, and not for the first time.

Once back down off the scree field, I reconnoitered, carefully studying the map, not wanting more of that kind of adventure—but there was more to come, unbeknownst to me. In fact, it would be a day that would test my commitment to life, but in a slow steady way, kind of like backing off that mountain. It would also test my commitment to reality. I eventually found the right road and continued on to the base of the peak.

Redcloud is not a particularly difficult peak, as peaks go, but all Colorado peaks require stamina and being in good shape. And you can die on any of them if things are just right—or wrong, I should say.

The Silver Creek route up Redcloud follows the creek for a few miles, then veers off onto the flanks of the big peak into tundra and eventually on up the summit.

It's a pleasant hike up the creek, and the climbing actually begins in earnest after leaving the drainage. It's about nine miles roundtrip with an elevation gain of 3700 feet.

Because of my false start, it was now getting late, only about an hour before noon, which is when one should actually be on top of the peak, not starting out, for the monsoons can carry you off the top if you're there when they come in, and they almost always come in.

The sky was clear, though I know how quickly clouds can form in these mountains, but I started out anyway. I could turn around if things got bad, no problem. But I had seriously discounted one factor—my own tendency to be compulsive.

My daypack had water, a jacket, and gorp. I hiked quick, strong, to the base of the peak, the altitude making me somewhat light-headed. On and on, through stands of willows, through fields of boulders, until I could see the ridge high above that led to the final summit.

I had to stop often to catch my breath. Clouds were forming, but didn't look too serious. I continued on.

I finally reached a small saddle, and by now the winds were whipping around me. Tendrils of clouds moved in, and the temperature dropped.

I climbed upward, upward, as it became darker and darker, and by now it was early-afternoon. I stopped to catch my breath again.

The snows began. I heard a rockslide above me, but couldn't see anything, and it soon quieted. Now, eating gorp, drinking water, I could feel my strength go, and I had to now decide whether or not to continue.

I had put on my somewhat light jacket, but was getting chilled anyway. The prudent part of me said turn around, but the compulsive part said go on.

So much effort, so near the top—the urge to continue is strong in a situation like this, you have so much already invested. Decisions often aren't prudent, especially if pushed by determination. I decided to summit.

My decision was accompanied by even darker clouds and an immense sense of urgency, dread, and deadly compulsion. Later, my brother told me of climbing the same peak and rescuing a climber who was hypothermic and had no idea who he was or even where he was, and who was thinking about going back up instead of down.

It wasn't long till I was on the top, but there was no reward, no view, except that of swirling snow and black clouds. I'd never felt more alone in my life.

I wanted to stop, to sit, like I always did on top, but the sense of urgency wouldn't go away, it was now even stronger. Retreat quickly, it said. The winds began to howl.

It was a long hike back, as the altitude and effort had taken its toll. The retreat down became a test of willpower, and now I began to shiver.

Hypothermia set in, the biggest killer in the mountains, and I hadn't come prepared with enough warm clothes in what could be a fatal error, especially when hiking alone.

I continued to eat gorp on the way down for energy, but I was failing and becoming fatigued beyond what I should be, and my core body temperature was dropping.

My legs felt like lead, and I wanted more than anything to stop and rest and take a quick nap. I knew I had to continue, by now I was running only on determination.

I had heard the many stories, I knew how easy it was to die like this. Snow swirled around me and it was nearly dark, not from sunset but from the thick black clouds.

I began to lose my sense of who I was and where I was and why I was there. For a bit, I thought I was being followed by a cougar, but it soon melted into the swirling snow.

I stumbled on, and I thought my brother was with me and began talking to him. But somehow, deep within, I knew this wasn't right, that I had to keep going, that something was very wrong.

I felt dizzy and stopped for a bit, leaning against a tall pine, wanting nothing more than to sit down and take a nap. I was overwhelmingly sleepy from the hypothermia and altitude.

Finally, I sat down. I just wanted to take a quick nap, and then I'd get up and continue on. Last thing I remember was how quiet the snow seemed to fall, how quickly it was changing the color of my jacket from blue to white.

When I woke again, I felt very strange. I had no idea how long I'd slept, and I also had no idea where I was. I'm not sure I even knew who I was.

My toes and fingertips were numb, and the edges of my ears had a strange burning sensation. I remember a strange musky odor. I thought I was sitting in a rocking chair, and I tried to stand up, but couldn't, and it was then that I realized I was being carried.

I finally regained some sense and remembered who I was and what I was doing there. Someone had found me and was carrying me. It felt like I was thrown over someone's shoulder, and this seemed odd to me, but then I thought, well, how else would you carry someone?

I tried to talk, asking, "Who are you?" and received no reply. We just continued on down the trail. I recall feeling very warm where I was in contact with this person, and I thought they must have a high metabolism to have such body heat. It helped warm me up a lot. It felt like they were almost burning hot.

As I became more aware of my senses, I realized that whoever was carrying me was quite large, and the ground wasn't very close below me. It was then that I really paid attention, and looking down the backside of whoever it was, I noted that they were indeed big.

I could see the huge muscles in their legs moving as they walked, and they didn't seem to have any trouble at all carrying me, and I'm 6 feet and weigh a good 200 pounds.

Things began to dawn on me very slowly, maybe because I couldn't believe what I was seeing. This person wore no clothes, was covered in dark brown hair, and was barefoot!

I could make out their tracks behind us, and they were huge, at least twice what mine would've been, pushing deep through the snow (which was now a good six inches in depth) and pressing on into the ground beneath.

I now began to question my sanity. I must be dreaming! How could something like this be? I'd heard of Bigfoot, or Sasquatch, but it was a myth, a legend, and not in Colorado, but rather in the northwest, like in Oregon and Washington.

Strangely enough, this allowed me to relax. It was just a dream, and maybe I was even dying. The brain did strange things when it's freezing, so I imagined, anyway.

But all of a sudden, my survival instinct kicked in. I didn't want to die. I had people I cared about and things I needed to do. I couldn't just passively let myself die out here. I had to pull myself out of this hallucination and come back to reality. I needed desperately to get back to my Jeep and get warm. I started yelling and kicking, and I tried to twist myself loose.

Next thing I remember, I was being gently placed onto the ground. I lay there for a moment, afraid to look up.

What if this wasn't a dream?

When I finally opened my eyes, I saw I was on the ground next to my Jeep. I slowly pulled myself up and looked around. There was nothing there, nothing out of the ordinary, just me and my Jeep.

I fumbled with my pack, which was still on my back, and found my keys.

I'll never forget how difficult those last few steps were, it was all I could do to unlock the door, get in, start it up, turn on the heater, soak in the heat. It felt as hard as climbing that entire mountain had been.

I finally relaxed, savoring the warmth, still wanting to sleep. But the snow was still coming down, and I now began to worry about getting stuck. I had to get out of there!

Was it a dream? A hallucination? I had to make one last attempt at making sense of it all, so I opened the car door and looked out, but nothing was there, just swirling snow.

I was too weak to get out and look around for footprints, plus I was totally weirded out at that point and half-terrified.

I grabbed a sack from the passenger side that contained what was going to be my dinner: bread, lunchmeat, apples, and some cheese. I took the sack and placed it outside next to the car.

If the creature was real, I owed it my life. I yelled out, "Thank you!"

I knew at this point I must be crazy, throwing away my only food and yelling into the storm. What if I got stuck and needed that food?

The sense of urgency was now even greater, so I drove away, half-numb, but coherent enough to make it on down to Lake City.

In town, the sun was shining, the sky blue, but the mountains behind were gone, hidden in black clouds.

I later heard that the San Juans got over two feet of snow that day and on through the night, storm raging in an anger that seemed malevolent. I had a fierce headache for two long days. My ears, toes, and fingertips suffered light frostbite.

But what suffered most of all was my idea of what made up the natural world. In fact, that's never recovered. I know the creature saved my life, if it was a real thing and not a hallucination, but I'm still afraid now to go out into the woods alone, though I'm OK with others around.

I went to my cousin's house in Lake City and then to the doctor, where I was treated and released. She believed my story, though I didn't tell her for several days.

The next summer, we decided to go back up there to get some closure. When I got out of the car, it was a beautiful sunny day, but I still flashed back to that snowy day. It felt like I was back in the storm, and I kind of panicked. She put her arms around me and just held me while I cried, and I'm a grown man.

Was it a dream? I'll never know for sure. But I believe it wasn't, based on the musky smell of my clothes, and more convincingly, on a small bit of dark hair that had caught in the zipper of my pack when the animal was carrying me.

I've placed this in a small bag, and in a weird way, it's kind of like a treasure, for it helps me to remember that there are other intelligent caring animals on this big planet.

God bless that creature, whatever it was, for it saved my life that day.

[3] The Beast on the Peak

I really enjoyed guiding Howard on several flyfishing expeditions, and I hold his storytelling abilities in high regard. Too bad you can't hear him tell the story, because he was really good with the spark and drama. He had everyone around the fire really entranced.

Howard has since passed away, but his story goes on. He really enjoyed telling it, and I first heard it while drinking beer with him and several others after a great day fishing the Yampa River in northwest Colorado. Howard was a great guy, and I wish I had seen those photos he took.

I've been retired some ten years now after spending some 30 years as a microwave technician for the government. You can see I'm no young guy, and it's a wonder this episode didn't give me a heart attack.

My job was to maintain the microwave sites across the Four Corners region of the Southwest. I routinely traveled to the mountain tops where these sites are located in Colorado, Arizona, New Mexico, and Utah.

For the first 28 years of this job, I worked alone, until the government made a decision to have us guys always work in pairs.

Here's the story behind that, told for the first time ever, which I can do now that I'm retired. If there hadn't been other witnesses, I would've probably been retired early on a medical disability for being nuts. And I would probably have to agree with that assessment.

I seriously doubt if anyone will believe this story anyway, but here goes.

Being a microwave communications technician involves more time spent getting in and out of sites than actually being there, because usually the roads are gnarly and rough and windy and steep and exposed.

Winters were the worst time to go into these sites, as you can imagine, as they were invariably on mountain tops, but I had to go when things went down, regardless of the season.

I would go in with a vehicle, usually a pickup or Suburban, until the roads got snowed under, then I'd pull a trailer with a Snowcat on it, get as far in as possible, then unload the cat and drive it on up to the site.

I often saw some of the most beautiful sights imaginable, going in like that, things like entire forests covered in thick hoarfrost after a storm, things you don't see at lower altitudes.

Anyway, it was mid-winter, sometime in January, and I'd been sent to a big peak in southeastern Utah, one of my sites, but one I seldom visited, as the equipment there was fairly new and rarely needed work. That was fine by me, as I didn't much care for the road up there. It was steep and scary.

The views were spectacular, though, and I always enjoyed looking out over the desert, it was like being in an airplane.

I knew it had been snowing over there, and a call to the county road-maintenance guys confirmed I wouldn't be getting in very far without the cat, so I loaded up the Theikol and headed out, getting into the nearest town by late afternoon, which was standard operating procedure, as few of these sites were close to headquarters.

I got up early the next morning and was soon in the cat, heading up that damned steep road to the top. I hadn't seen that much snow for several years. It had really dumped up there, and that road gave me fits, but I finally got in to the site.

Our microwave communications sites never used to be fenced, but there are now so many people everywhere that the government has put high metal fences around them with locked gates.

But at that time, there was no fence, and a good thing, as the snow was so deep up there that one would've had a rough time getting in through the gate. Just too much snow.

I finally got up there and pulled the cat up next to the building to assess things, to see how to get inside. Because of the snows, all these buildings housing the communications equipment have doors in their roofs, as well as the sides.

There was no way I was going in the side door. I couldn't even see where it was. So I climbed up the ladder to see how much snow I was going to have to shovel off before I could get inside. Like I said, most of my work was getting in and out of the sites. Once I was there, I usually could reset or fix whatever wasn't working within a few hours at the most.

Well, I can tell you that what I saw sure wasn't what I expected to see. No shoveling necessary, the door was already open.

These buildings are all metal, and the metal door had been literally wrenched off its hinges and was lying on the roof, twisted from the force. It looked like a pretzel. This was a fairly heavy door.

I went and looked down the ladder into the building, and it had quite a bit of snow inside, enough that I couldn't get in there to fix anything. It didn't look like anything had been damaged, and the snow was probably what had caused the equipment to go off-line.

I then walked around a bit, trying to figure out what had happened. I knew there was a logical explanation, and I suspected some sort of weird microburst, kind of like a tornado.

These big peaks get winds like you wouldn't believe, and there was a Snowtel up on this one that had recorded winds of over 100 m.p.h. the winter before, so that's exactly what I suspected—a freak wind had somehow caught the door, even though it was firmly closed and locked, and pulled it off its hinges, twisting it in the process. A strange-but-true-tales candidate.

After looking around a bit, I decided there was nothing I could do by myself. I needed help getting all that snow out, and we needed a new door. It would take a couple of guys easily several hours to clear the building before I could even see the equipment to work on it.

So, I resigned myself to heading back down the mountain and having to come back again.

I got on my radio and called out to headquarters, telling my boss what was going on. He agreed that it would be a waste of time for me to try to clear the building by myself, especially since the next storm would just bury everything again with no door. I should go home, and we'd get a crew and come back in a few days, along with a new door.

I sat down on the edge of my snowcat's treads to have lunch and a hot cup of coffee from my thermos before heading out. It was cold up there, but a beautiful blue sky made it seem warmer. The air was so crisp that you could see individual ice crystals floating around.

I carried a camera with me and often took photos of some of the beautiful country I got to see on my travels. After lunch, I pulled out the camera and climbed back up on the roof, thinking this might be a good thing to document, just to show people what the wind can do. I took a few photos and then climbed back into the cat, fired it up, and headed back down the mountain, following my tracks.

I wasn't more than 100 feet from the top when I saw that something had walked directly in my snowcat tracks, something large—and not very long ago. I hadn't been up on top more than an hour.

I stopped and got out, wondering what would be up here. Bears would be hibernating, and cougars would be in lower climes, as would about any other animal with any sense.

I stood there with my jaw hanging open for some time. The tracks were huge. It looked like someone had been walking along my cat tracks, someone with bare feet. Big feet. I felt kind of spooked, to tell you the truth.

The only critters I've ever seen on those mountains in the winter were birds. These footprints had a stride that was really big, maybe four feet between tracks, and that made me stop and think, I can assure you.

I had recently seen a TV show on the Abominable Snowman, and I was thinking this could be it, right here in Utah.

I remembered my camera and took about a half-dozen photos of the tracks, putting a glove next to them for scale. I estimated them to be a good 16 inches long and about 10 inches wide at the ball of the foot, tapering to a narrower heel that was about five or six inches wide.

My snowcat was heavy and had packed down the snow pretty good, yet these tracks sank down even deeper, a good six or eight inches into the packed snowcat tracks, making me think the critter was quite heavy.

I was getting more spooked by the minute, as the tracks were going downhill, the same direction I was going. I got back into the cat and continued on, hoping I wouldn't run into this thing, and I have to tell you, I drove slow.

After about 50 feet or less, the tracks veered off into the forest, heading straight up the road bank, where you could see it had slid backwards a bit, as the bank was steep. Even at that it was up that bank in three steps, a good 15 feet.

I got off that mountain as fast as I could, and it wasn't until later when I was telling my wife about it that I really got the heebie jeebies. She asked if maybe what left the tracks was what had ripped up that door.

I took the film to the grocery store to be sent off for developing, and decided it was a bear that had accidentally come out of hibernation early and had ripped up the door looking for food. A really big bear. I didn't say anything to my boss or anyone else, we'd see what was there when we went back.

It was a Thursday when I came back home, so we didn't go back until the following Monday. At this point there were three of us, me, my boss, and another technician. We were going to go back up there and replace that door and get that site back online.

We tied the heavy metal door onto the side of the cat and squeezed in and headed up the mountain. There hadn't been any fresh snow since I'd been there last.

I was watching for tracks all the way up, and when I got to that last 100 feet, I don't know what I was thinking, but they were gone, of course. I'd run over them on my way down.

But the tracks going up the bank were still there, just as I'd left them. I stopped the cat and got out and showed them to the guys. Of course, they weren't as fresh, but they hadn't melted any and were pretty distinct.

Nobody knew what to make of them, and Jerry, the other technician, who also liked to carry a camera, took some photos. This was good, it meant I wasn't the only one puzzled by it, and now I had corroborative photos. But they weren't nearly as impressive as the other pictures I took had been, as the toes were missing from where the animal had slid a bit while climbing.

When we got on top, everything was just as I'd left it. Nobody could figure anything out, it was just too bizarre, but we set to shoveling and eventually had the building cleared. I worked on the equipment while the other guys fixed the door, no easy task.

We were finally done and ready to roll. We'd worked right through lunch. I think nobody wanted to be there any longer than necessary. The place just felt kind of foreboding. We finally locked the door and loaded up, heading back down the mountain.

I was watching for more tracks, but didn't see any—until we got partway down the mountain, that is, and then I'll be darned if we didn't find more! Same deal exactly, right in the cat tracks.

We stopped, and by now we were really beat, but Jerry and I got out and took some photos. Our boss, Tom, didn't have a word to say and just sat in the cat.

We got back down to the parking area and locked the gate behind us, then drove over to where the pickup and snowcat trailer were parked. It was dusk, almost dark at this point, it had been a long day. We just weren't prepared for what we saw next.

The pickup tailgate had been wrenched from the truck and thrown a good 20 feet. I say thrown, because one couldn't see any drag marks, and it wasn't carried, as there were no tracks in the snow.

To make things worse, the cat trailer had been, at least so it appeared, physically picked up and twisted, wrenching it and the hitch into a mass of twisted metal and separating the trailer from the truck. Around everything were more of the huge tracks like we'd seen up on the mountain.

We just stood there, tired—exhausted, really—and didn't know what to do or say. But I can tell you we all had the fear of the devil in us, we were scared. I suggested that we go to the motel and figure it all out and come back the next morning, and we could decide what to do then.

We wasted no time getting into the truck, but Tom didn't want to leave the cat. He was afraid something might happen to it, that whoever or whatever had done this would be back, so he drove it until we ran out of snow on the road, then parked it.

At that point we were a good five miles from the gate, so we hoped it would be OK. It was an expensive piece of equipment.

Back at the motel, nobody said much. We went to dinner and then just went to bed, all kind of in shock, in our own rooms.

The next day, we went back and got the trailer and jerry-rigged it up and managed to get it into a welding shop and have everything fixed enough to travel, it and the truck both. We then went back and got the snowcat and headed home.

I don't think any of us ever mentioned it to one another again, but it wasn't long until a policy came down from the muckity-mucks that solo travel was no longer allowed. They cited health and safety reasons.

Tom never did ask me to go up to that peak again. I'm not sure if he ever went back himself, either. Nor Jerry.

I retired a couple of years later, and I still have the photos of those tracks in my chest of drawers, no closer to knowing what made them than the day it happened.

[4] The Rock Clacker at Buckhorn

I sometimes guide women on my flyfishing trips, but usually they're the wife of one of the guys, along just for the fun instead of the actual fishing.

But Leslie was a different story. She loved to fish, and I think this may have come from going up to the lakes with her grandparents when she was a kid, as she recounts in her story, which is one that really boggles my mind.

Leslie told this story around a campfire high at the edge of the Flattops Wilderness area in western Colorado, an area that's had a number of Bigfoot sightings, and an area that figures prominently in the last story of this collection, as you'll see. But her story happened a bit of a ways away, down by Montrose, Colorado

This incident happened to me when I was nine years old, at Buckhorn Lakes near Colona, Colorado. I typically would spend a lot of time with my grandparents in the summer, as both my parents worked.

My grandfather liked to be outdoors, and even though he didn't fish, we often went to nearby Buckhorn Lakes in the mountains to picnic and hang out. On this particular trip, my grandparents had me, my two cousins (boys, aged 11 and 12), and two teenaged boys who were staying with my aunt and uncle while their parents were gone. I don't recall where my aunt and uncle were that the boys were all with us, but I would guess they were probably working.

The road up to the lakes is really rough and it takes awhile to get in there. We rode in the back of the pickup. This was back before anyone thought much about that, but it did have high side rails and was pretty safe, considering. This is when it all started, on the way up to the lakes.

I was a bit of a tomboy, and now that they had older reinforcements, my two cousins decided it would be fun to pick on me, which they often did anyway. They were half afraid of me because they knew I'd get even—usually later, when they least expected it.

But now, they started in earnest, teasing me and trying to get me to stand on the side rails of the pickup, which they, of course, weren't afraid of doing. I thought it was dangerous and stupid and told them so.

They countered by telling me I was a chicken and flapping their arms while making chicken noises, you know how kids do.

This kind of thing continued all the way to the lakes, where we all got out and were sidetracked by the picnic my grandmother made.

After lunch, we all decided to go down to the biggest lake and see what we could find. My grandmother was reading a book, and my grandpa was taking a nap in his camp chair, typical for both.

Nobody worried much about us being out and exploring. We knew how to take care of ourselves, could swim, and were pretty woods savvy. That's just how it was back then, how I grew up, we weren't coddled and had a lot of freedom.

So off we went to the lake, which was long and narrow, a typical mountain lake in the trees, with logs floating near the shores. I don't remember much about what we did, just the usual exploring and things kids do with their endless curiosity.

It wasn't long before we decided to float some logs around the edge of the lake, pushing on them with long sticks, and that soon led to us taking off our shoes and getting onto the logs and floating around. Not a real safe thing to do, really, but we all could swim.

It wasn't long before I was again being teased. The boys could all go faster on their logs than I could, as I was smaller, and they eventually ditched me, leaving me to float alone on the far side of the lake while they hightailed it back to camp. I was pretty mad, but I just couldn't keep up with them.

At that point, I decided it would be best to get off the log and walk back around to camp, so I got off. The foliage around the lake was pretty thick, and I remember getting scratched up by some kind of bush with thorns, probably wild rose.

My shoes were back where we'd got on the logs, so I was barefoot, and this made things harder. I was also constantly having to climb over logs and push through tree limbs, and it wasn't long before I was lost.

I turned back the way I'd come, thinking I'd catch sight of the lake and continue following the shore, but there was no lake where I thought there should be.

I kept trying to head for the lake, but I'd just get into thicker vegetation and be even more lost. I started yelling, hoping someone would hear me, but there was only silence.

After about a half-hour of this, I was scared and sat down, crying. I'd come to the edge of a deep ravine, and I knew there wasn't a ravine near camp, as we'd hiked around there a bunch on other trips. I knew I must be some distance away.

I had no idea what time it was, but I knew my grandfather usually liked to head back to town around four p.m., as he always wanted to get back in time for the evening news. He was a news junkie, plus my parents both got off work at five.

I was now worried they would leave me up here, an irrational fear, I realized later, but when you're just a kid and you're scared and alone, you worry about such things.

I also remember my grandmother telling us once, if you get lost, just sit down, and eventually someone will find you. Don't wander around, you'll just get more lost.

So I decided to just stay where I was and wait for someone to find me. I started yelling again, then it occurred to me maybe a bear or cougar would hear me and come and get me, so I shut up, even more scared.

It seemed like I sat there forever, it really did. Every little sound in the woods terrified me, even though I'd been in those same woods since I was a baby. We'd been coming up to the lakes for years. But when you're all alone and lost, things change pretty rapidly and in a major way.

I kind of hunched myself under some logs and big ferns, then realized there were ants all over, so at that point, I decided to try to climb the nearest tree and see if I could make sense of where I was at.

Like I said, I was a tomboy, and I was good at climbing, so up I went, no trouble at all. If I remember, it was a large aspen tree. It seemed like I was way up there, but I think in retrospect I was only about 15 feet up, clinging to a large branch and sitting on another, my bare feet dangling down.

I just sat there, thinking at least now I could see if a bear or something was coming, or if someone was coming to rescue me. For some reason, it made me feel more in control of the situation, though I really wasn't.

I just sat there. Again, it seemed like forever, thinking about what it would be like if nobody ever found me. I'd given up on yelling, but kept straining to hear if anyone was calling my name.

It wasn't long before the daylight seemed to change, the sun was getting more oblique, and it was getting along late afternoon. Now I wondered if everyone really hadn't left me and gone home, and I started crying again, to myself though, quietly. Some sense of survival told me not to advertise my solo nature to the woods. I was also getting thirsty.

All of a sudden, I could hear somebody coming through the woods, towards me. I wanted to yell out, but something said not to.

The footsteps crunched on the leaves, and they were coming straight my way. I hoped and prayed it would be my grandfather. It sounded heavier than one of the boys would sound.

I could finally make out what was coming, a little bit, and I knew it wasn't my grandfather—it was a bear! It was dark and big and hairy all over. After this realization, I became terrified and pulled my legs up into the tree, hiding as best I could behind branches and leaves.

The bear came right under me and stopped. Its head was right under me. I could've reached down with my legs and kicked it.

I remember thinking it smelled awful, it really really stank. I almost threw up, it was so strong, like rotten eggs or worse.

Strangely enough, I was more scared when I saw it coming than when it was under me. I can't explain it, but I felt a sense that it wouldn't harm me.

Did it know I was right above it? I had no idea, it had just stopped there and was standing, it didn't look up at me at all. I held my breath and hoped it would soon leave.

After a few minutes, it walked a few feet away to a little clearing and sat down on its haunches. I could now really see what it was, and it wasn't any bear like I've ever seen.

My young brain couldn't figure it all out, so I decided it was some kind of new species of bear, or maybe one that had developed wrong. I was only nine years old.

The creature had the same color as a bear, a dark brown, but it had massive shoulders like a football player, only bigger. Its muscles rippled underneath its skin. I still couldn't make out its face, as it had its back to me, but it had a large head with shoulders that kind of just melted into the head, no neck at all, and the head seemed shaped kind of like a football, but not as pronounced. The fur really didn't look like fur, but rather like hair, and kind of hung off the arms, which were long and powerful looking.

It just sat there on its haunches for a bit, then it reached over and picked up two large rocks and started banging them together, making a rhythmic sound, like someone on a drum or something. It had a definite rhythm.

It knocked the rocks together so loud that I thought they would break. They made quite a noise. Then it would pause and listen. After a few rounds of this, I could hear yelling way in the distance.

Now I was getting scared. What if it was calling in its friends, telling them I was there? I was terrified and started crying again, though I tried not to.

The creature just kept banging the rocks, and the replies in the distance seemed to be getting closer and closer.

The yelling was now nearby, but I couldn't make out what or who it was, but it was definitely human. I wanted to yell back, but I was too scared. I just clung to my tree, and the creature just kept banging the rocks together.

But it wasn't long before the yelling was close enough I could tell it was my grandfather and cousins. At that point, the creature stood up and turned around and looked straight up in the tree at me. It had known I was there the whole time.

As it stood there looking, I could easily make out its face. People have asked me what it looked like, and all I can say is it looked almost human, but not really, as it had its own looks. It had brownish-gray skin all on its face, except hair on the cheeks and chin, kind of like a man would. It was big, and its dark-brown eyes had no white to them, nor did I make out any ears, just hair all over. And its eyes were very clear and intelligent.

I was still terrified, but yet I now knew it wouldn't harm me. After a moment, it turned and walked into the forest the opposite direction of the yelling. It was gone in a second, its large muscular legs carrying it, gliding like the wind.

I now began to yell, as I could hear my grandfather was really close. He and my cousins were soon there, helping me from the tree.

He then asked how I had managed to make so much noise, and I told him a big brown animal had done it and pointed at the two big rocks.

I don't remember much else, except we went back to camp, and it was almost dark when we got to the truck. My grandmother was very relieved to see me.

Nobody scolded me at all, and even the boys were nice to me, they had retrieved my shoes. I rode in the cab all the way home, still in shock so much I couldn't even talk to answer my grandmother's questions.

A few days later, my grandfather asked how I could've possibly made so much noise with the rocks, as that's what had led them to me. He said he'd noticed that the only rocks there were big, and I would've had trouble picking them up, yet alone banging them together. I'm not sure he really believed me about the big animal, but the rock clacking was a point in my favor.

My cousins believed me instantly and told me I'd seen a Bigfoot. After that, they seemed to be kind of in awe of me, and all the teasing stopped.

We still have family get-togethers once a year or so where we see each other, though we never talk about that day.

[5] Happy and Hoss

This is one of the more unique stories I've heard, though it wasn't told around a campfire. Joplin, the storyteller, was a friend of a friend who agreed to tell me his story when he found out I was collecting Bigfoot tales.

Is it true? I don't know, but he swears it is, and he carries a photo of Happy in his billfold and has invited me to meet the dog. I'm inclined to believe, based on his personality, good sense of humor, occupation (a teacher), and my friend's good words about him. It's quite the tale.

My story happened almost 10 years ago. I live in a small house on the edge of the timber near Chehallis, Washington. My little farm house has a very nice porch, and I like to sit out there in the evenings and read and drink tea. I've done this for years. I'm a middle-school teacher.

I have a big white dog I call Happy. I don't know what breed he is, but he's all white and has long hair. I suspect he's part Newfoundland, though he's not quite that big.

Happy's name fits him, he's always wagging his tail and putting his head in your lap. I love that dog, and I worry, 'cause he's getting old. But how I came to have him is a story I won't tell anyone except under complete anonymity, it's just so unbelievable. But here goes.

I didn't always have Happy. It's not like I got him as a pup or anything. One evening in the summer I was sitting out on the porch when this big white dog came into the yard, then right up onto the porch, wagging his tail.

Of course, it was Happy, and I petted him and tried to see if he had a collar with tags. No collar.

I figured he was a stray, so I decided I'd give him something to eat, then figure out what to do, maybe take him to the animal shelter if he stuck around and didn't go home.

So I went into the kitchen and got him some leftover meatloaf. He seemed like he was really hungry, like a stray would be.

He wasn't particularly skinny, so he hadn't been lost long, if he was lost and not just wandering around. I gave him plenty to eat, and he curled up by my feet and went to sleep. I kind of liked him from the very start, even though he stank to high heaven.

I went back to my reading, when I noticed some motion from the corner of my eye, out at the edge of the forest. I figured it must be a deer. I watched but didn't see anything.

But Happy perked right up. He started wagging his tail and took off into the trees. OK, I thought, he must be with some kid out exploring or something, or else he likes to chase deer, maybe that's why he's lost. I hoped he'd now go on home, problem solved. I didn't think anything more about it.

A few days later, the same thing happened, Happy showed up, very hungry. I was a bit put out at his owners for not feeding him, but I gave him some dinner. That time, Happy spent the night. I made him a bed out on the porch because he still stank.

I began wondering if my feeding him wasn't going to turn him into my dog, when he already had a home. I liked Happy, but I didn't particularly want a dog at that time.

My previous dog had recently died, and I was pretty distraught over it, and I just didn't want to go through that again. A lot of people use this as an excuse to not get another dog, not that it's a very good one, as there are lots of dogs needing homes.

So this time, Happy stuck around for a few days, and I gave him a bath. Then he again disappeared. This kept happening, Happy would show up starving and smelly, hang around, then disappear.

By then I'd given him his name and kind of resigned myself to having a part-time dog. I'd grown attached to him and decided I wouldn't take him to the shelter if he did ever stick around, but keep him. He's just such a sweetheart.

So, one particular time, Happy and I were out on the porch, and he'd been here for a few days. He was a gorgeous dog after I would bathe him and brush out his coat, very pretty.

Happy had been just laying around, but he suddenly got up and started wagging his tail. But this time he stayed on the porch. He just stood there.

I figured I knew what was up, the kid who owned Happy was back for his dog, and I wanted to talk to him about this situation. So I sat there and watched for him.

Nothing, but Happy still stood there wagging his tail, like he was glad to see the kid, but really wanted to stay with me.

So, I called out, "Hey there, is this your dog?"

No sound or movement, but Happy was still wagging his tail. Now I could see someone over in the trees, but it didn't look like a kid at all, it looked like a grown man. This worried me a bit. I expected him to call out for the dog, but he just stood there. I called out again, but no answer.

The longer the guy just stood there, the more uncomfortable I became. I went into the house, but Happy wouldn't come in, even though he was now a housedog. He just stood there, wagging his tail.

I watched out the window, and this thing stepped out of the trees and started walking towards the house. I can't describe my feelings, but it was a total fight or flight reaction. I ran for my .22 rifle.

By the time I got my rifle, this creature was almost to the porch. I'll try to describe it: it was about five feet tall with hair all over it, except on its face, where it had brown skin. It had broad shoulders, and its head seemed to come to a bit of a crest.

It had no neck and massive shoulders. Its arms were long, and it had a very muscular torso. Its face was almost human, with broad cheeks and a pushed-in nose.

I was terrified, but Happy was still wagging his tail. It didn't occur to me until later that the creature meant the dog no harm.

All I could think of was that he was coming after Happy, so I shot through the open door. I got it square on, and I shot it twice before it turned and ran, screaming. I'll never forget that scream.

I was beside myself as I watched Happy run after this creature. I called to him, desperate, but he ignored me.

What could I do? I ran after Happy, trying to catch him. I loved him and didn't want him to come to any harm. I still had my rifle. I was torn between not wanting anything to happen to Happy and being scared to death and wanting to hide.

I remember running as hard as I could though the thick foliage, getting whipped in the face by branches, stumbling, but continuing on.

Until suddenly, I came upon Happy and the creature, and I came to a roaring stop.

The creature was lying in the bushes, breathing hard, and Happy was sitting by it. I stood there for a moment, about 10 feet away, and I suddenly felt terrible.

It just looked at me, and its left shoulder was splattered with blood. I could see the pain in its eyes. It made no movement towards me, just watched me, while Happy licked off the blood.

Oh God, I felt terrible, I had done this, and the creature had done nothing to me.

I didn't know what to do, I suddenly wanted to help it. It looked young, like maybe a teenager of that species would look. I knew I had to do something, but I was afraid to approach it.

I was suddenly so angry that I took my rifle, emptied the chamber, and started beating it against a tree, splintering the stock until it was useless, then I threw it into the bushes.

Then I started crying. The creature just watched me and did nothing. It was in pain.

It occurred to me that maybe it was thirsty. I was wearing a felt cowboy type hat, and there was a stream nearby, so I went down and filled the hat with water. I was afraid to go near the creature, but I did, showing it the water, and it took the hat with one arm and drank, spilling most of the water out. I went down and got more, and this time I held the hat while it drank. It began moaning.

I knew the wounds needed dressing, but I was afraid of it. What could I do? I decided I would try to help it anyway, I had caused this.

I ran back to the house. There, I got my little daypack and filled it with the stuff I would need to clean the wound, including my first-aid kit.

But how would I get the creature to lie still? It would be painful, and how would it know I wasn't just hurting it more and attack me?

I got several bottles of wine from my wine cabinet. Maybe if it would drink the wine, it would help the pain. I wished I had some hard liquor, but I'm really not much of a drinker. I grabbed a plastic pitcher from the kitchen.

I ran back, and believe me, I was pretty ramped up on adrenaline to even consider doing what I intended to do.

I ran down to the little stream and put some water in the pitcher, but I then filled it mostly with wine. I hoped the diluted wine wouldn't be as noticeable to the creature and it would drink it.

It was still thirsty, and the plan worked. I did this several times, and then I waited. The creature had now had a full bottle of wine, not a lot for an animal its size, but hopefully it would help the pain. Sure enough, it seemed to kind of relax and nod off a bit.

Did I mention how much it stank? It really put me off, but I knew I had to help it anyway. But as I tried to get close enough to examine the wounds, it was really awful, the smell.

But I worked through it, and managed to kind of clean where the two bullets had gone into its shoulder. The blood had begun to clot, and I put some Neosporin on it, then bandaged it.

The bullets hadn't been close enough to each other to create compound damage, and it didn't look like they'd hit anything but soft tissue, no bones, but it was hard to tell.

But the real question was, were the bullets still in it or had they gone through? I needed to move the creature, turn it over, to see what was going on. By now it was sleeping and was maybe even in shock. I wondered if the wine had been a good thing or not.

I finally grabbed the creature's left arm and slowly and carefully turned it over enough to see where the wounds were. It was heavy.

It looked like the bullets had gone on through, and I cleaned the wounds, put a bandage on them to keep them clean, then turned the guy back over. He stirred a bit, and I jumped back. Then he slept.

I didn't know what else I could do, so I went home. Happy chose to stay by the creature's side, which I was glad of, in case he needed protection.

So, I went home and sat down, or collapsed is more like it. I fell asleep in my chair. I think I was in shock.

I woke up in the middle of the night, worrying about the creature and Happy, so I got a light and went back out there. I took some food for Happy, then I added in some stuff for the creature, a big ham I had.

The creature was sitting up, and he looked like he was feeling a bit better. I say *he*, because I decided it had to be a male, as it had no breasts. The rest is just conjecture.

Happy was sitting by him, and this creature was actually rubbing the dog's neck! And I had thought he was going to kill him. Once again, I felt like a total jerk.

I was still very scared of him, but I decided to call him Hoss, since he was so big, even if a youngster. So I called Happy over and gave him his dinner, which he was happy to get. Isn't Happy a great name?

I could tell that Hoss was interested, so I then offered him the ham, I carefully held it out to him. He took it with his big hand and ate it in just a couple of bites. I handed him some water in the pitcher, and he drank it. His eyes were glazed over, and I knew he was still in a lot of pain, so I once again poured wine in with some water and offered it to him, and he drank it.

I don't remember much after that except waking up in the morning, I'd gone to sleep in the woods with Happy and Hoss.

Hoss was again moaning, and I knew I needed to do something besides giving him wine all the time. I tried to tell him I'd be back by motioning with my hands, then I went home.

I drank some coffee. I still couldn't eat. Then I found some medicine I'd had from when my previous dog was sick, Tremadol, a morphine-like painkiller. I had quite a bit, as he'd been on it for a spine-degeneration problem that was ongoing. I got some more food and went back out.

I fed Happy again, then offered Hoss some steak from my freezer, not even thawed out yet. He ate it, although he seemed to act like he wondered what the heck—he knew it was meat, but he'd never had a meatsicle.

I then offered him some raw hamburger I'd had in the frige, but I'd put Tremadol in it, having extrapolated how much by guessing his weight. It took a good bit.

He ate it, and it wasn't too long before I could see him relax. I wanted to again clean the wounds and put fresh bandages on, and I hoped he'd let me. He actually did, like he knew what I was doing, and even moved around a bit so I could get to his back.

I cleaned up the wounds. The bleeding had stopped, and they looked better, but now I remembered that any time my dog had a wound, the vet had used antibiotics.

I began to worry about infection. How in the heck was I going to get antibiotics for Hoss? Just tell the doctor I was treating a Bigfoot?

Yes, by now I had decided Hoss must be a young Bigfoot. And now you understand why I don't tell this story to just anyone. They would have me committed.

I was exhausted, so I went home. I hadn't been home ten minutes when I thought about Hoss being out there in the sun, needing water, so I went back out with my patio umbrella and a bucket.

I got this all set up, left a big bucket of water, and went home again. I was glad I was a teacher and on summer vacation and didn't have anything else going on. I lay down to take a little nap, but couldn't sleep.

I think this is when the fantasy nature of everything hit me. I began to wonder if I'd gone mad. I got up and paced around.

I needed to talk to someone, but who? Everyone would think I was totally insane—yup, you shot a Bigfoot and now you're out there nursing it, you and this big white dog. I lay back down and finally went to sleep.

This went on for days, me taking food out and nursing the wounds. Happy stayed with Hoss the entire time. I worried about what would happen if someone found them, but the forests here are so thick, and this was really off the beaten path, and fortunately that didn't happen.

Slowly Hoss began to improve, and it really wasn't long before he was up and about, but unable to use his arm to hunt or whatever he did for food, so I would continue to bring him stuff.

He was beginning to eat me out of house and home, but I didn't mind. I brought him all kinds of food, but he liked meat and berries the best, which made sense, I guess. Maybe he ate kind of like a bear or something, lots of berries and plant matter and meat when it was available. I have no idea what Bigfoot eat when on their own.

But it wasn't long before he was getting his own water and all that, but still, his left arm was hanging like it was paralyzed or something. That really worried me, how in the world could I adopt a handicapped Bigfoot? But at least the wounds never got infected, and they healed nicely.

We'd been into this for weeks now, but I could see that finally his left arm was beginning to regain movement, and eventually he seemed to be able to use it.

Finally, Happy began coming back home with me, and Hoss often wouldn't be there when I came out to feed him. I would leave the food, and it would be gone the next day.

One day, after I'd been out there several days in a row and the food hadn't been taken, I stopped feeding him. I knew he was gone.

The few very trusted people I've told this story to always ask me about my relationship with Hoss. Did he learn to communicate with me? Did he seem to hate me or to appreciate my care?

In short, Hoss seemed to just take what I offered and never showed anything much like we'd call emotions. As I became less afraid of him, I began to realize that he'd been just as afraid of me.

We both developed a mutual respect, and I think when I destroyed the gun, he knew what I was doing, and it let him know I meant him no further harm.

No, we had no communications, other than I did see him clap his hands a number of times when he saw me after his arm had healed, like oh boy, dinner.

He did seem to have a sort of goofy smile, where he kind of bared his teeth like a chimp would do. At first it scared me, then I realized what it was and would smile back at him.

He had big square teeth, like a human's, only much bigger, and no canines. But other than that, it was much like two humans who couldn't talk to one another and just did the business they needed to do.

What really got to me, though, was watching how he and Happy interacted, just like a boy and his dog.

Once, about three months after I had quit feeding Hoss, we were out on the porch and Happy took off, wagging his tail. I knew he'd seen Hoss, and I wondered if he'd come back. I half hoped Hoss would show himself, but he didn't.

Happy came back a few hours later, stinking to high heaven. But I never saw anything like that again, it seems that Hoss left after that, maybe he was saying goodbye to Happy.

I don't know, maybe he reunited with his parents. They probably thought he was telling them tall tales when he told his side of the story.

I know I still haven't really processed all this, even ten years later, and probably never will. I still often wonder if I didn't hallucinate the entire thing, but I know it was real. Hallucinations don't go on for weeks, and something sure cleaned out my freezer.

If Happy could talk, I know he'd vouch for my sanity.

[6] A Night of Fear

This story was told to me one night by a woman named June while at, of all places, a bar in St. George, Utah. She was the wife of one of my fishing clients. So this isn't really a campfire tale. But given her story, I doubt if it will ever be told anywhere but indoors.

I'm 43 years old, and I live in Las Vegas. This story happened to me five years ago. I'd be glad to take a lie detector test if anyone doesn't believe me, but I don't suppose anyone will take me up on it. I do know how strange this story is, but it's true.

It was in northern California that all this happened, not far from the Trinity Alps. I've since found out there are a lot of Bigfoot accounts from there.

My ex-husband and I had just split up, and it was a nasty divorce. I had been suspecting he was losing his grip on reality for several years, and things kept deteriorating. I'd rather not go into it, but I ended up letting him have the house just because I didn't want to fight him. I was afraid of him. I just wanted to get away at that point.

So, I had given my husband the house, and I was renting a small apartment. I got a call from a mutual friend of ours telling me that my ex had gone to the police and filed a report accusing me of identity theft.

Apparently he'd maxed out his credit cards and was going to use this as a way to get out of paying them, plus get back at me.

Like I said, he wasn't doing very well at that time using his faculties. He's since been institutionalized for other things he's done (like threatening to kill his boss).

I eventually got the house back and sold it, so I'll add right here that things have worked out OK for me. There were no charges filed against me. I've since moved from that area.

But after I got that call, I had no idea what would happen, and I was scared of him. He could say or do anything. The police might believe him, and it could take a long time to vindicate me, and I didn't want to spend any time in jail.

I've never been in trouble, so I didn't understand how it all worked, that I could get an attorney and fight it, I just thought I'd be sent to jail. I guess I was a bit naive.

My job was only part-time, so I decided to let the apartment go, put my stuff in storage, and hit the road for a bit until things settled down.

I hadn't been served with any papers from the police, so I wasn't bailing on anything. I just knew what my ex was up to.

It was just a few weeks later that I found myself camped near the Trinity Alps. I'd bought a small tent, a camp chair, a Coleman stove, and everything I needed to camp out.

I was kind of enjoying it, as it was the first time in years I'd had any down time, and I'd really been through a rough time with my ex. I needed a break. I had forgotten how consoling nature could be.

I was in a small campground out in the middle of nowhere, and there were almost no other campers. A few people would come for a day or two, then leave. I usually had the place to myself.

I had been there one week, and I knew I would probably have to leave in about a week and find another place, since the rules said two weeks, as it was public land. But I was enjoying it and intended to stay there as long as I could. No one I knew had any idea where I was.

The first few nights were a bit scary, I'll admit, and every little noise would kind of make me worry. I was afraid of bears, mostly, but I had bear spray with me.

I wasn't armed, and I will add that I will never camp again without being armed—but I'll just never camp again, period.

As I got used to the night sounds, I got more comfortable with being out there and began to really enjoy it. And when people were in camp, it's doubtful they knew I was alone, as I was camped in a spot where you really couldn't see anything but my car. The tent was hidden in the trees.

On about the eighth night, things began to happen. At first, I could hear sounds that were new to me, the first being the sound of a baby crying far off in the trees, and that sound turned into more of a wailing. That really freaked me out, but I decided it had to be a mountain lion. It wasn't anywhere close by, and I knew cougars are afraid of people unless they're habituated, like in rural areas with houses in their habitat.

So I settled down and was a bit wary, but was OK and went to sleep. Nothing else happened that night.

The next night, I could hear what seemed to be some kind of big animal sighing. It sounded really big, but it wasn't close by.

It would just go huhhh, huhhh, like you would when you were trying to get someone's attention without actually saying something. I got my bear spray ready, but nothing happened.

The next morning, I contemplated leaving, but it was such a pretty place, and I didn't know where to go, so I stayed. Things didn't seem so scary by daylight.

The third night, I could hear what sounded like someone hitting a tree with a big stick—whack, whack, whack— three times in a row.

Not long after that, I heard the same thing, but in a different direction and further away. This went on for a few minutes, and I admit, I got up and sat in my car, trying to figure it out.

I finally decided it must be deer whacking their antlers on trees. I finally got out of the car and went to bed.

Then, sometime deep in the night, I woke to what sounded like pebbles being thrown onto my tent. I was scared to death, but managed to get out my flashlight and shine it around from inside the tent flap. I was too scared to get out.

I thought I heard something running away. I decided it was a raccoon that had been in the trees, knocking sticks onto my tent.

It's funny how when you don't know about certain things you can figure out ways to explain away the deeds they do and sounds they make. It will become clearer what I'm talking about in a minute. I lay there and finally went back to sleep.

You can imagine how fast I jolted awake when I woke up to feel my tent, with me in it, being pulled, scooted actually, across the ground.

I screamed, and whatever it was let go of the tent and took off. I could hear the sound of something large running through the trees, and it sounded like it was on two feet.

I was petrified with fear, but I finally got up the courage to get out of the tent, and I jumped in my car. Whatever it was, it had hands, no bear could've pulled my tent like that. And it was very strong, as I weighed about 150 at the time. It pulled everything up like it weighed nothing, and I had the tent staked down.

I knew it was time to leave, but I realized I'd left my keys in the tent. I was too scared to get out and go get them, but I knew I had to.

I jumped from the car, crawled into the tent, grabbed my keys and pocketbook and jacket, and jumped back into the car. I left all my camp gear.

It was then I saw the pair of eyes glowing in the dark, a greenish color, right on the other side of my tent, a good eight feet off the ground.

I fumbled for a minute, then started the car up and tried to accelerate out, but it didn't move. I was panicky, why wouldn't the car go?

I then realized there was something behind me. I could make out a dark silhouette in the rearview mirror. There was more than one of these things, whatever they were!

Just then the car began rocking up and down, up and down, like something heavy was jumping on my bumper. I panicked, really stepped on the gas, and whatever it was, it must've let go, because I spun out, throwing rocks into the air, nearly losing control of the car, rocketing forward, and almost hitting a tree.

I was now heading down the little road out of the campground as fast I could go. I finally got out onto the county road and started picking up speed, when I noticed something coming up right next to the car, running beside me.

Even though it was dark, I could make it out, and it scared the crap out of me, it was so big and massive. It had shoulders a good four feet wide and a huge head, and it was a dark color.

And what really scared me was that it was keeping up with me, even though I was now going fast! How fast? I don't know, I was too scared to look at anything but where I was going, but I know it felt like a good 30 miles per hour or even a bit more, which was fast given that I was on a rough dirt road.

Now there was another on the other side of the car. I felt like I was having a nightmare, this couldn't be happening!

The one next to me started slapping the car window, like it was trying to break it or else make me panic so I would wreck.

I stepped on the gas even more. I was going way too fast for a rough dirt road in the mountains in the dark, but I didn't care.

I came to a curve and skid around it, nearly running over the one on the other side of me, and that's when I lost them.

I drove and drove and drove. I drove until I was nearly out of gas, then stopped behind a grocery store and got out of my pajamas and into some regular clothes, got gas, then drove some more.

I didn't really stop for a good ten hours, and by then I was exhausted, so I got a motel.

I didn't even really know where I was going, and I couldn't eat. I couldn't rest, and I couldn't sleep.

The next morning, I stopped at a store and bought some new clothes and threw my old ones away, including the pajamas I'd been wearing, trying to get rid of anything that would remind me of that night.

I drove some more, and got a different motel in another town, but I still couldn't sleep until it was dawn of the next day, then I just collapsed and didn't wake up until the maid kept pounding on the door.

I finally figured out where I was, and I wasn't that far from my old hometown, back in Idaho. I guess my instincts had taken me there, even though my mind was pretty much gone.

I barely even remember anything about those days on the road. I went on into town and found a cheap apartment. I knew I would have a lot of thinking to do.

It was literally weeks before I was able to go out and drive around town much, before I felt like I was getting kind of back to normal.

I finally looked up a couple of old friends, and even though I never told them my story, I did tell them about the divorce, and they helped me a lot, thinking that was the source of my trauma.

I eventually went to a shrink, but they refused to believe that night was real and tried to treat me for hallucinations, so I quit that.

I'm pretty much OK now, but I refuse to go out into the woods, ever. I moved to Las Vegas, as far from forested country as I could find, here in the middle of the desert. I will never set foot in the woods again, or camp, for that matter.

As far as that night goes, I know it was real, and I can show you the deep marks all along the driver's side of my car, like something with very hard nails had scratched it.

I'm going to keep that car forever so I'll always know I wasn't crazy that night, and that something real happened to me.

[7] Fire on the Mountain

This great story was told around a campfire deep in the heart of Bigfoot country, at an annual gathering of flyfishing guides near Eureka, California. It definitely put a chill into all of our hearts, especially knowing Wayne would never fabricate anything and had a heart solid as gold.

I'm Wayne and my friend Eric is the other person in this story. Eric would vouch that this story is 100% true, if I knew where to find him. At the time this happened, we both lived in southern Colorado, near the San Juan Mountains.

Eric and I were high school buddies, and we've been through hell and high water together. Eric dropped out in the eleventh grade, but I finished and went on to college and got a degree in geology.

I then came back to our hometown and became a high-school science teacher at a private school. Eric never did much of anything, working part-time for his dad at his mechanic shop, but not even working most of the time, just bumming, living with and off his parents.

Anyway, after I started teaching, Eric had a lot of free time and I didn't, and Eric was always trying to get me to go do things with him when I didn't have the time.

I felt kind of bad for Eric, as he seemed to be steadily going downhill. He was a smart enough guy, but just couldn't put his life together.

His mom called me once in awhile, asking me what to do for Eric, but I never could answer that question.

All this leads to why we were camping high in the San Juan Mountains when we should've been home, snug and warm in our houses.

It was mid-September, and Eric had started drinking. His mom called and asked if I knew what would help him. I didn't.

Not long after that, Eric called and was bemoaning that we never did anything together any more. I decided it would be a good time to go climbing. We had both been into climbing when things were better for Eric.

I had the week off, since the school kids were out doing their annual fall outdoors exploration trip, and I didn't have to go along. I had already done my duty on the spring trip (the school was very big on outdoor education).

So, I proposed that Eric and I hike into the Grenadier Mountains, a very rugged range in the southern San Juans, and do some climbing.

Eric was very excited. We had talked about doing this for years, ever since we were in high school.

We got our backpacking gear together, along with food and supplies, and headed for Durango, where we would board the Durango-Silverton Railroad. The only reasonable access into the Grenadiers was on this tourist railroad, via a route called Elk Park, and backpackers were common on the train for this reason.

The train would stop at the trailhead and let people off, also picking up whoever had come out that day. The train was on a tight schedule, so you'd better be there if you wanted a ride out.

It was a pretty good way to do things, and the train had been accommodating hikers and climbers like this for years, for the price of a train ticket. The Forest Service had built a bridge across the Las Animas River, the only safe place to cross this fairly swift stream, and this is where the train stopped.

So, Eric and I got off the train, hitched up our packs, crossed the bridge, and were on our way. There was a lone hiker who got off after we did, but we were soon ahead of him. It was a beautiful sunny day, and the weather forecast called for good weather all week.

The first four or five miles of this hike are up a drainage that gets steeper and steeper, on a very grueling trail that leads along a deep valley and that eventually comes out by some beaver ponds.

We had planned to go on up into what's called Vestal Basin, at the base of some immense and wild 13,000-foot peaks we wanted to climb (one was called Vestal Peak).

But there was no way were we going to make it to the basin in one day, we were both out of shape and the trail was too rough.

When we finally came to the upper end of the valley, we found enough grassy space around the beaver ponds to pitch our tents, and there we camped for the night, exhausted.

I remember waking up in the middle of the night to the call of an owl in the distance, thinking it was interesting that owls were up this high, as we were nearing timberline.

Things got more interesting when the owl seemed to be right over my tent, as if it were in the tree right above me. It was loud and kind of freaked me out, but it soon stopped, and I went back to sleep.

The next day, we were both stiff and sore, but we soon walked it out, heading on up the trail. I did notice that there was no tree above my tent and wondered about that owl.

After several even more grueling miles on a very steep trail covered with ball-bearing rocks, we eventually came to Vestal Basin, a beautiful high-altitude basin with a small pale-blue glacial lake in it, called Vestal Lake, appropriately enough.

Vestal and Arrow Peaks towered high above us, making us feel very small. We were in rugged country, country one should respect, as it cared not one bit if you lived or died. We seemed to be the only people up there.

We powered up my little backpacking stove and made some hot dinner, some kind of freeze-dried chicken stir fry, then had hot cups of tea, which seemed to perk us up—it was probably the sugar.

The stars were unbelievable, and I told Eric that the moon would be full tomorrow night. We could see its light arcing up over the mountain to the east, but we went to bed before it actually came up, tired.

We slept well that night, in spite of the thin air. We were at an altitude of about 11,000 feet. The next morning we were up early and got ready to climb. We wanted to climb both Vestal and Arrow, although we knew it probably wasn't going to happen in one day, as neither of us were in that great of shape.

It was a beautiful day, and even though we only made it up Vestal, we felt great to finally be doing something we'd talked about for years, to climb in the Grenadiers. We would climb Arrow tomorrow.

We sat on top and talked for a long time, talked about Eric's life, and what he was going to do to change things and get back on course. I knew Eric enough to know he needed encouragement, but that when we got back down he would lapse back into his old ways.

The day ended with another fire and a different freeze-dried menu entree, this one beef stroganoff, which really wasn't half bad. We skipped the tea and were in our little backpacking tents before the sun had even really set, it was still twilight.

I had wanted to stay up and watch the moonrise but was just too tired. The altitude and climbing will do that to you. I've slept for 12 or 14 hours after climbing. You just can't get enough oxygen at those high altitudes, and you get tired from the physical exertion.

I woke to a glowing light all around me. The full moon had risen. It was so bright I could see the outline of my pack where I'd laid it next to my tent.

I wasn't sure what had awakened me, but now I could hear that owl again, and it just struck me as very odd. It was in the distance, over towards the base of Vestal Peak. I had to go to the bathroom, so I got up and stepped out of my tent.

I walked around to the back of the tent and did my business and was crawling back in, still half asleep, when I could hear Eric say, "My God, Wayne, get over here, now!"

I could see him kind of leaning against a large rock next to his tent, so I went over there. I'd had no idea he was up. He grabbed my arm before I could even say anything, and I could tell he was upset.

I could see where he pointed in the moonlight, his arm waving over towards Vestal Peak in the distance. That was where the owl was also hooting, off and on.

What I saw made my hair stand on end. I actually started to shiver in the cool night air, I was so scared.

The whole base of the peak shimmered with ghostly creatures, shimmering and wavering and moving back and forth. I can't even describe it, it was so unreal. It was something right out of a horror movie, and we looked to be the victims. There was no place for us to go, to run and hide.

Eric just stood there, quietly saying "What the hell," over and over and over. I could tell he was beside himself. I just stood there next to him, not believing what I was looking at. I'm a geologist, a scientist, for God's sake, I don't even believe in ghosts.

Finally, something kicked in, and I realized the figures weren't doing anything, they were just repeatedly shimmering and wavering in the moonlight, but the movement was fairly consistent and predictable.

It then dawned on me that we were seeing the moonlight reflecting off of millions of crystals on the mountain, which was made of volcanic schists full of reflective mica.

I relaxed, the adrenaline dropping, and told Eric what we were looking at. He cussed a bit, then relaxed.

We then watched the spectacle for a bit, knowing we were looking at something most humans had never seen, nor would see. It then became somewhat of a wonder to look at. The fear was gone.

I have no idea what time it was, maybe midnight or one a.m., and we decided to go back to bed. The owl started in again, and I asked Eric what he thought of an owl way up there. He noted that he felt it was strange, but probably not unheard of.

We both stood there for another few minutes looking in the direction of the owl, which was the same direction as the "ghosts"—when we both saw it, apparently at the same time.

"Shoots," Eric commented, "There's somebody walking around over there."

We could both make out a dark figure against the glowing crystals, or rather, we could see movement. The distance was enough to not be able to clearly make out what it could be.

It was big, because it appeared to be up against the mountain base, where the glowing rocks were, which wasn't that close, maybe a quarter of a mile away. We both just stood there, watching, and we knew this wasn't an illusion created by moon and rocks.

The figure walked back and forth for a bit, and we could hear the owl faintly hooting from the same direction. It really gave me the creeps, to say the least, and I had no idea what it could be.

Our optical illusion that the glowing rocks were ghosts was just that, an illusion, but we both knew that this was real. Too real.

"We need to get out of here, now," Eric whispered to me. "Now," he repeated. He seemed terrified.

"We can't go anywhere in the dark, it's too dangerous. We have to stay here, we have no choice. What do you think it is?"

"It's something big, I know that, and it's no bear, it's walking on its hind legs, it's bipedal."

I crawled into my tent and got my Ruger pistol, which I rarely carried with me, but had worried a bit about bears and decided to bring it.

"We have this, don't forget," I whispered to Eric, showing him the gun.

I'd never seen Eric so riled up. This was the beginning of my realization that he really had deteriorated into a very fearful person, not at all like when we were in school together.

But I can't say I blamed him right now, I was pretty concerned myself. This was just too weird. And now there was another owl hooting, over to the right of where the figure was. Soon we could make out two figures in the moonlight.

Eric wanted to hide somewhere, get away from the tents. I talked him into staying put, on the premise that we were safer out in the open, where we'd pitched our tents, rather than back behind rocks or trees where we couldn't see around us.

We needed to just stay put. I decided whoever it was knew we were here, anyway. They had probably heard us talking. We would just stay here and watch and listen.

We took turns going into our tents and getting dressed while the other one stood lookout. I took my cell phone out of my pack. No service, but I had suspected that.

I checked my gun to make sure it was loaded, and I put extra ammo in my pockets. We wouldn't go down without a fight—assuming whatever it was, was even interested in us, which I had no evidence of, other than the weird owl hooting above my tent the previous night.

Eric pulled a bottle of rum from his pack and was proceeding to drink it. I decided to let him go ahead, he was of no use anyway, as scared as he was, and maybe it would relax him. He was becoming a liability. He soon crawled into his tent.

I settled against a large rock, gun in hand and headlamp on my head, ready to turn it on at a moment's notice.

I was angry at Eric, he had chickened out when I really needed him. He was not someone I would ever backpack with again or trust.

I was tired and wasn't sure I could sit there all night keeping watch while he slept, drunk. I guessed they could have him first, but I knew I could never let anything happen to him.

I sat and watched. I could see the two figures, and they were now just standing there, not moving, as if they were watching me. It then dawned on me that I wouldn't have the moon as my ally much longer, it was beginning to set in the west, much earlier than it would in town, since the high peaks were blocking it. It would soon be pitch dark.

I needed a plan. I've never been so scared in my life, but I'm proud that I didn't collapse like Eric, and I was able to carry on.

It then dawned on me what that plan would be. I furiously began collecting pieces of wood, running back and forth from camp to the edge of the nearby sparse bushes and Krummholtz. I could see well enough in the moonlight to not turn on my headlamp.

Every once in awhile I would check back to see if I could still see the figures, which I could. I had no idea what I would do if they came over to our camp, except to start shooting.

I soon had a huge pile of dead wood. As soon as the moon sat, I would light it, and hopefully it would get us through until dawn, if I were careful.

I made some rocks into a fire ring near the tents, then dragged the wood within distance of the fire so I would at no time be unprotected. I could just reach for wood without leaving the fire. All this activity helped take my mind off the situation.

I then sat back and waited for the moon to set. I had no idea what time it was, but it was late, and I was exhausted. The figures continued to walk back and forth over under the mountainside. I was beginning to doubt my own sanity.

As soon as the moon set, I lit a small fire, sitting as close to it as I could, facing outward, gun in hand. Eric's tent was nearby.

I sat there until dawn, totally terrified, praying, barely having enough wood to get through the night. I never heard nor saw anything of the two figures, though I thought I heard voices several times but wasn't sure.

As soon as I could see well enough, I started packing up my tent and gear, exhausted. I woke Eric up and he started doing the same, as groggy as he was. After a short time, I heard someone talking, and I turned to see the lone hiker standing nearby, the same guy who had gotten off the train when we did.

He sat down by the extinguished fire, shivering, then began to tell me of being stalked all day yesterday by something really big, something that would walk in the bushes nearby parallel to him and yet never reveal itself.

He had thought it was a bear, and finally decided to climb a rock face that no bear could climb. He was a solo climber and had come to climb Wham Ridge, a nearby giant slab of rock that's famous in the climbing world.

He sat there all night, a good 100 feet straight off the ground in a niche in the vertical cliff. He could see our fire, but decided against trying to make a break for it.

Two figures were below him, trying to figure out how to get to him. They had actually climbed within thirty feet or so of him, then would slip back down.

He heard them calling like owls until they had finally left at dawn, and that's when he made a break. He couldn't really see them, except to see that they were huge and dark.

They were not bears, but rather stood and walked on their hind legs. And bears don't hoot like owls. He was shaken and wanted to leave, but not alone.

We were soon all three on the trail, not stopping for anything. Going back down the first part of the trail was extremely dangerous for us, as we were tired, in a hurry, and the ball-bearing rocks and steep trail were just as hazardous as when we came up.

It was very frustrating, trying to hurry, and yet being afraid of slipping and falling off the trail. It took us hours to get back to the railroad tracks. We arrived a good hour ahead of the train, so we made some lunch and had some tea, exhausted.

When the train came, we were happy to be back on board, surrounded by happy talkative tourists asking questions about how our trip went and how beautiful it must be up there and asking if we'd seen any wildlife. We just smiled and nodded.

I never went into the Grenadiers again, nor did Eric, as far as I know. The event did seem to sober him up, and he ended up going to a trade school, where he studied, of all things, culinary arts. He went on to be a chef, and that's the last I've heard of him.

The other fellow we met has continued to be a friend, but we've never backpacked or climbed together. I gave such activities up, except for the outdoor trips I take my high-school students on, and believe me, we'll never go near the Grenadiers.

[8] The Green River Ghost

. . . .

The fellow who told this story was a good friend of my dad's and has since passed on. I'll never forget him telling this story to me and my brother as kids.

It really scared the bejeebers out of us, and it's partially responsible for my interest in Bigfoot. He always swore it was true, as did his lovely wife, Helen.

My name is Jeb, and I'm a retired engineer on the railroad. I'd like to tell you a little story about a very unusual thing that happened to me one frosty night on my run between Grand Junction, Colorado and Helper, Utah.

Specifically, this happened in Green River, Utah, about midway through the run. It's not a long or spectacular story, but it's one that still causes me to wonder what I hit that cold November night.

We had a long train that night, and we were carrying coal. I don't recall how many cars we had, but we'd picked up from Grand Junction and were heading west, coal that had come up through Delta from those mines over by

Paonia. I remember it being an unusually long train, and we had two engines on the front and two helper engines on the back.

I was glad I didn't have to take it up over Soldier Summit, as I knew it would be a long slow night for that engineer. Instead, I would be in bed in Price, Utah, at the end of my run.

Nothing unusual happened as we dragged all that coal out of Junction, on through Ruby and Horsethief canyons along the Colorado River, and then on up the adobe hills into Cisco, Thompson Springs, and then on past Floy as we got closer to Green River.

I always enjoyed going through Green River. It's a little desert town that reminded me of Roger Miller's song, "King of the Road." It seemed like it was stuck in the 60's.

I always liked to slow down a bit when we were coming around that big sweep that goes under the highway there on the east side of town, 'cause I knew we'd soon be crossing a road with no railroad signal, and I didn't want to run into anybody.

Last time I was there, that road out to the little airport, it still had no signal, you just looked both ways and then drove like hell, hoping no trains were coming.

Just after the big sweep, before the train reached that crossing and the old train station, you crossed over the old bridge across the Green River, there by the golf course, which used to be an old river meander. That railroad bridge has been there for many years and is still going strong.

So, it was about 2 a.m., and I'd hit the brakes just a bit to slow 'er down, just as we came around that big sweep.

Now, it takes a helluva lot to slow a big coal train down, so my braking was more a matter of my own psychology than reality, I liked to feel things were safer, but they probably weren't. I couldn't have stopped that train on a dime if someone's life depended on it, which I would soon find out.

We came on into the sweep, and I could see the lights of town to my right, where there's a strip of motels. Now the sweep straightened out, just in time to cross the bridge, a classic old structure with several metal spans, the kind you see in vintage railroad movies.

And just as we straightened out, I could see something walking on the tracks ahead, going away from me, something large, and it was right in the middle of that bridge. I hit the panic button and the brakes, but there was no way in hell I could stop in time. I also got on the whistle.

The train came upon the thing quickly, and I could make out a very large figure that looked like a football player, it had huge shoulders and a massive head. It looked human, but somehow not.

I was on it fast. It stopped and turned towards the train, and I could see a huge dark face with dark eyes.

I felt sick as the engine hit it. I hoped it wasn't a human, and I didn't think so, because it felt more like we'd hit a large bull, and yet it seemed to be something upright and walking, and that face seemed intelligent, what I could see of it.

We had hit it straight on, as there was nowhere for it to go on that bridge, no place to step off to the side. I felt it, and I was sick. I've unfortunately hit deer and elk, and only a big bull elk would be even close to that kind of impact.

My brakeman came up and asked what was going on, and I told him. I called the guy in the helper engine and told him what was happening, to watch and see what we'd hit.

I then radioed headquarters, all the time trying to stop that damn train. I didn't get it stopped for a good three-quarters-mile, way out beyond the town, into the desert.

Headquarters radioed that they'd stopped all traffic and that I was to back up and stop in town at the old station and wait. The sheriff would be there to meet me. So I did.

It took awhile to get that train backed up, and I realized as I was backing that this would put the back part of the train right back on the bridge, and I didn't want to do that. It needed to be left clear so they could see what had happened, if anything was there.

So I radioed back to headquarters and got permission to stop out of town and wait.

We sat there all night, what was left of it, stopping all railroad traffic, while the sheriff investigated. We couldn't get out and go anywhere, because it would've been a long walk in the desert, no roads and a few deep arroyos to cross, so we just sat there in the train.

We finally got word to back up onto the siding there, where the sheriff could examine the front of the train, and that we would soon need to be on our way, as we were holding everything up. So we did.

By now it was early morning. I got out and met the sheriff, and we examined the front of the train. It had a big dent, which is hard to do to an engine.

He told me that they hadn't been able to find any sign of anything or anyone, whatever it was had to have been tossed out into the river.

They had searched all around the bridge abutments and everywhere, with no luck, and he had sent some guys down the river in a boat to look. But except for the dent in the engine, we had nothing.

We were then given instructions to proceed, so we did, and I switched out in Helper and my wife picked me up and I went home to Price.

I didn't figure I'd ever know what I'd hit, but it sure as hell traumatized me. I wanted to quit. I didn't think I could ever forget seeing that figure come into my lights and the look on its face just before I hit it.

I had to make a report, and I just said it looked like something big, like a huge bull. I didn't mention the upright stance or that face, people would think I was crazy. There's no human being on this planet that big.

The railroad gave me a leave of absence when I asked for it, and I took two weeks and went up to Scofield Reservoir and fished. That seemed to do the trick, and I started feeling better.

I was soon back to work, but every time I crossed that damn bridge I had to distract myself, look out at the water or at the motel lights, because I would think I could see its face. That would really get to me.

Finally, one night about a year after the accident, I decided to just deal with it, to face my fears head on and just go across that bridge without thinking about it.

So when I got close to Green River, I just looked straight on, and I could finally see that silver metal bridge glowing in the moonlight. I just kept with it, watching. I was determined to just get over this thing.

As the train came over the bridge, I'll be gotoheck if it wasn't there again! Everything was just like on that night before. I hit the brakes and panicked and hit the whistle, bracing for the impact. But there wasn't any impact. Nothing.

The brakeman came up and asked what was going on, and I decided to tell him. He asked if I'd been drinking, but he knew I was damn serious. He just shook his head and wrote it off to having a flashback, and said he'd keep it between the two of us.

I was shook up, but kept on going, and when I got to Helper, I told my wife all about it. She was concerned, and told me I needed some time off.

Anyway, to make a long story short, this happened to me every time I went across that damn bridge, and I knew it was the ghost of that thing I'd killed.

I spent many hours actually crying over that whole incident, and I got to where I was afraid it would somehow follow me home. I asked for a new route, but there weren't any available, so I finally took an early retirement.

And I'll be damned if the brakeman didn't call me one day and tell me he'd seen it himself. And I've even heard a few stories about the guys playing golf there, when they get to the part of the course that's next to the bridge and it's late evening.

So I know it wasn't just my overactive imagination. I just hope it never comes up this way.

[9] Snowball

I met Jay one afternoon when I got good and stuck on a backroad in western Colorado. It wouldn't have been too bad, but I had three fishing clients with me who were pretty green, and they thought they were going to die out there, even though we were on a well-travelled county road.

Jay is an exploration geologist, and he came up and pulled us out with his nice Ford 350 company pickup. I invited him to come have dinner with us that evening, which he did. We all got to talking around the campfire, and here's the story he told.

I grew up in Deer Lodge, Montana, where my parents have a cattle ranch. After I graduated from high school, I went to Montana Tech in Butte, just down the road about 30 miles.

I always wanted to be a geologist, and that's where one goes to study for that in Montana. I'm now working for an oil exploration company in Colorado.

Anyway, I met the gal who would become my wife in Butte, she was also studying there. She became a geological engineer, but is now staying home with the kids for a few years. At the time of this story, I had no idea she was to become my wife, or this event never would have happened. I would've just gone on home and waited for her to call me.

It was summer, and I was working on the ranch. I helped out in the summers, as my parents needed me. I was almost done with school. I would go back to school in the fall to start my fourth and last year there.

I always went go see my girl and future wife, Kay, in Butte on weekends, I'd go see her Saturday morning and go back home Sunday night.

Well, this particular visit didn't go too well. We went out to that casino in the old part of town for a late breakfast. Those casinos have the best and cheapest food around, so we always went there.

That's when Kay told me she wanted to start dating other guys, she wanted to be sure I was the right guy for her. She felt we were both too young to be so hooked on each other. We needed to shop around more, so to speak.

I was really shook up, but I agreed it was an OK idea and left. I didn't want to date anyone else, I knew she was the one. I'd been out with enough women to know that.

So I just told her to go ahead and date and call me when she was ready to go out with me again, if ever. Assuming I hadn't found some other girl by then, that is. I was pretty mad.

So I just got in my old pickup and headed home, back to Deer Lodge. I realized later I had forgotten to give her a ride back to her apartment, but by then it was too late, I was on down the road, and I figured I'd never see her again anyway.

I got part-way back when I felt the need to be alone. I didn't want to go home and explain everything to my parents as to why I was back early.

I always carry emergency gear in my truck, and I had my sleeping bag and some water and some chips and beer and a few candy bars, so I just decided to head out and spend the night out in the mountains camping. It would be good for me, like the old days before I met Kay, when I camped a lot.

I don't want to give the exact location of where I got off the freeway, but let's just say it's a nowhere exit, there's no town there, just a road going up into the mountains. A lot of western Montana is like that, freeway exits that give access to hunting and ranch roads.

This particular road crossed the Clark Fork River and went through a lot of beautiful cottonwoods down in a valley, and there's a big cattle ranch there. It's a really nice place and the owner was a family friend, a long-time rancher there.

I thought about stopping, but I was in no frame of mind to talk to anyone, so I just kept going on up the road, which soon left the wide valley and started up the mountain into the Beaverhead-Deerlodge National Forest.

I didn't want to get up there too high, 'cause then I'd be in the deep timber, and I've always liked being able to see out a bit. And most of western Montana is grizzly country, and I sure as hell didn't want to meet one of those guys.

So I went up a few miles and pulled over at the edge of the woods into a clearing. There were cattle lounging around in the shade, and I noticed the ranch had put out salt licks for them there.

A small creek ran nearby, a perfect spot except for the damn cattle and their manure and incessant flies.

The cattle cleared out when they saw me coming, so I decided to just go ahead and camp there. Camping was no big deal for me, I would just throw my sleeping bag on a pad in the back of my truck, as it had a small camper shell on it.

I was protected from the elements and pretty much any bears or such, and I could crawl into the front through the window in the back of the cab if I needed to.

But it was way too early to think about going to bed, it wasn't even noon yet. I had most of the day all to myself to mourn and feel bad, which I needed, 'cause I sure as hell did feel bad. I was broken-hearted.

So, I set there awhile in the shade until the flies finally got to me, and then I decided to go for a hike. I would climb up onto a small cliff I could see that looked to be about a half-mile away and do some geologizing, that always made me feel better, looking at rocks. So I put my water into my daypack with the candy bars and headed out. I was already feeling better.

I was soon up on the cliff and exploring around, spending the better part of the day there, figuring out the geology and walking the contacts. I still had a dull ache where my heart was supposed to be, but I was kind of wondering what it would be like to date other women, maybe it wouldn't be so bad after all.

I started wondering if that cute girl in my historical geology class last semester would be open to the idea, and that perked me up a bit. I knew her name and it wouldn't be hard to find her when fall semester started.

I noticed it was getting on towards sunset, so I decided to head back, my pack now full of rocks, the candy bars and most of the water gone. I was starting to get hungry, and I wondered if I could make it to morning. If not, I could always just head home.

All of a sudden it just hit me what Kay had said and done. I think I'd been in a bit of denial until then, maybe a survival mechanism. But it just hit me hard when I saw the sun about to set, because usually we'd go sit on her deck together Saturday evenings and watch the sunset while eating homemade pizza.

And now here I was, out in the wilderness, hungry and alone, boom, just like that. Things had changed so fast I couldn't even process it.

I was suddenly really angry at her and the world in general. I picked up a big stick and started smashing it against a big tree, yelling and cussing, just as mad as you can get, letting off steam.

Then I sat down and started crying, which ended up being a wailing sound before I finally got a grip on myself. What if one of the cowboys from the ranch was nearby and heard me? I'd be really embarrassed. So I tucked it in and got up and started back to my truck.

It was really getting dark now, and even though I got my flashlight from my pack, I wasn't real sure exactly where the truck was. I began to feel really uncomfortable.

I forgot all about Kay, except to wonder if she would care when they found my body, either mangled by a grizzly or from the fall off some unseen outcropping in the dark.

I was a fool to have let the dark catch me, no wonder she wanted to look around for someone else.

I angled in the general direction I thought the truck would be, and was walking along when I first heard the sound. Something was in the bushes nearby, maybe 50 feet to my right. It was walking along, just like I was, but staying hidden.

I could hear it crunching in the brush, and it sounded like it was on two legs from the way the footsteps went. That would mean it wasn't a grizzly, probably, anyway, as they walk on all fours.

But what was it? Too big to be a coyote, and too noisy to be a cougar, and anyway, cougars go on all fours.

A person? No, nobody could see in the dark to walk through the bushes at the same pace I was walking without stumbling and falling. I wondered what all my wailing and noise had attracted.

I shone my light in the general direction of the sound and called out, but I could see nothing. When I stopped, it stopped, and when I started it started.

It totally weirded me out. I wanted to run, but I couldn't see well enough. The best I could do was to get back to my truck and get the hell out of there.

But It was so dark now that I had no idea where the truck even was. I wanted to stop and sit down and cry and let whatever it was have me. I was starting to just not give a damn anymore. It had been a hard day.

But I kept walking, and I just kept angling towards where I thought the truck was, until I finally hit the road. I was relieved, maybe the thing would go away now.

Then it dawned on me that I had no idea if the truck was above me or below me—had I possibly come out onto the road below where it was parked?

I had no way of knowing, but I did know I had to keep walking downhill, there was no way I was going back up into the forest. If I did and the truck was below me, I would never find it and would end up in even direr straights.

So I just kept walking downhill, shining my light back and forth, hoping to soon see the reflection of metal. And the footsteps continued alongside me in the brush.

I can't begin to tell you how scared I was, I've never prayed so hard in my life.

I had the most dire feeling, a feeling of true dread, that something bad was going to happen, and I couldn't shake it. I was nearly panicked, and I was kicking myself that I hadn't brought my deer rifle from the truck. I still had my pack full of rocks, and I grabbed a couple of those.

The road just kept going, until all of a sudden there was something standing dead on in the center of it, something big. I yelled out, scared, cussing at it, until I realized it was a steer.

It stood there for a moment, blinded by my light, then turned and ran—right towards whatever was stalking me.

I heard a loud and very deep growl, and all of a sudden, the steer turned back and nearly ran over me, terrified. Whatever was there was more frightening to the steer than I was, and that scared me even more, if possible. I will never forget the sound of that growl, it gave me chills.

At that point, I ran. I could now see the lights of the cattle ranch down the road ahead, maybe a half-mile or so, and all I knew to do was run like hell towards them.

And then I saw it, the creature. It outran me and came upon the road and doubled back, as if to catch me. It was huge, and a dull white, like it had white hair or fur. Its eyes looked to be a couple of feet above my head, and I'm six feet tall.

And those eyes, they glowed red, just like a light on a Christmas tree. It wasn't a reflection of my light, like you see with some animals.

As it came towards me, all I knew to do was throw the rocks at it, and I hit it. I bellowed like a bull when I threw those rocks, as a shot of adrenaline surged through me.

By then, the creature was nearly to me, but when the rocks hit it, it stopped. It just stood there, looking at me for a moment, and I swear the expression on its face was one of shock. I'm not making this up, and what I learned later confirmed that possibility. It then slipped off the road back into the bushes and disappeared.

I turned and ran, no way was I going to give it a second chance. I was soon at the ranch, pounding on the front door, gasping for air.

The door quickly opened, and I recognized Sid, the rancher. Sid had eaten many meals at my parents' house, and he was a good friend of the family. He looked really surprised to see me. I went inside and slammed the door, panicked.

Well, Sid's a good guy, and he told me to sit down, everything was alright, I was safe there. I hadn't said a word to him about what I'd seen.

He locked the door and then turned all the lights on outside, the big halogen yard lights. Sid acted like he knew exactly what was going on. He had three stock dogs, and they all sat there in the kitchen with us, quiet as could be.

I finally calmed down enough to tell Sid my truck was up the road and wouldn't start and would he mind giving me a ride back up there to get it? Maybe in the morning, since it was so late, I added, even though it hadn't been dark all that long.

Sid must've found this kind of suspicious, but he grinned. Then he said sure, I could just spend the night there in the spare room and we'd go get the truck the next day. He then asked if I'd had any dinner and started fixing me some bacon and pancakes.

I swear, bacon and pancakes have never tasted so good before or since. The stock dogs all got some, then Sid made another big batch and took it and threw it out over the fence. He said it was for the pigs, but no respectable cattle ranch has pigs.

Sid then showed me the spare room and told me I would be fine there, nothing would bother me, and to sleep in as late as I wanted, he'd have more bacon and pancakes ready for breakfast, then we'd go get that truck.

He told me I should get some sleep, 'cause I was white as a ghost, and he was a bit worried about me.

I lay there in bed, trying to rehash what had definitely been the strangest and most stressful day of my life. I felt like someone in a weird film where nothing makes sense. In fact, I wasn't even sure I hadn't gone nuts and wasn't in the loony bin.

I had no bearings, no reason to believe anything was normal in any way, so I just went to sleep. I later had nightmares about the whole thing, but that night I slept like a baby. I felt very secure there with Sid and his stock dogs. Sid was one of the most competent and trustworthy ranchers in the area.

The next day, after breakfast and coffee, we went out to get my truck, and I saw huge footprints in the dirt roadway, like someone walking barefoot, someone really huge.

I looked at Sid to see if he noticed, and he just smiled. When we got to my truck, he waited while I started it and said he was going to follow me back down to make sure it ran OK. He never even asked what was wrong with it, it had started up just fine.

So, Sid followed me back down to the ranch, and when we got there, he pulled up next to me and got out. He leaned up against my truck and told me that it would probably be for the best if I didn't talk too much about what I'd seen last night.

I was surprised, and said so, asking him if he knew what I'd seen. He replied that sure, all the guys on the ranch knew about old Snowball, that's what they called him. Snowball had been around for years, and had never harmed anyone, though nobody trusted him much, and it was standard operating procedure to not go anywhere unarmed.

When I told Sid how the creature had started coming for me, Sid said that Snowball probably hadn't meant me any harm, he was probably concerned for me.

I felt incredulous, but Sid said Snowball had never actually harmed anyone, other than scaring them half to death. I figured Sid was just trying to make me feel less afraid.

He told me the creature had been there for at least 10 years, and everyone on the ranch knew about him, but it was an unspoken rule to not mention him to anyone else.

They would even leave him a deer each year during the fall hunt to kind of tide him through the winter, though Snowball never stuck around. Where he went they didn't know, maybe he hibernated, but he always came back each spring.

I was soon on my way, feeling like I had just hallucinated the whole thing. I went on home and spent the next week just doing my chores around the ranch and then sitting in my room each evening, staring at the wall. I told my parents I was sick.

I had decided reality wasn't what I'd thought it was, both as far as Kay went and as far as the natural world went. I wasn't prepared for the thought that Kay would give me the boot, nor that there were friendly Sasquatch near Deer Lodge, Montana—or any kind of Sasquatch anywhere, for that matter. I felt like I was lost at sea and had no idea where to turn.

Finally, about a week after the incident, Sid showed up at our ranch and asked if I wanted to go into town and have lunch. I really didn't, but I said yes anyway just to humor the old guy. It turned out to be a good thing, because we sat and talked about Snowball for a long time.

Sid told me lots of stories about the Sasquatch, and invited me to come back out to his ranch, which I did. I didn't see Snowball, but I did talk to some of his hands about it, and this finally helped me get a grip on the whole thing.

About two weeks later, Kay called me. She'd been busy dating other guys, and she was ready to concede that I was the real deal, and she missed me.

I was kind of put off at first, she'd hurt my feelings, but the sound of her voice melted everything away. I was at her apartment that very evening, where she told me how sorry she was and how much she cared.

We got engaged and were married the day after we both graduated from college.

I never told her about Snowball, honoring Sid's request, plus I knew she'd think I was crazy. I went back out to his ranch a year later, and Snowball hadn't showed up after a particularly hard winter.

They figured he had gone to that great Sasquatch Hunting Grounds in the Sky, and said they kind of missed the old fellow, even though he never hung around the ranch much, just to be fed occasionally when Sid threw food over the fence.

Kay and I both got jobs in Brazil, of all places, doing mineral exploration. We were away from Montana for several years, but when we finally returned, I saw Sid one day in Deer Lodge.

He informed me that Snowball had come back and had been looking pretty gaunt, but they soon had him fattened up with bacon and pancakes.

Sid said I should come out sometime and visit, he'd make me a batch. But it's a bit of a drive from Colorado, where we now live.

I heard later from my parents that Sid had passed away.

[10] Hotshots

This is a short but very poignant story. I met Cassie one evening when my fishing clients decided they wanted to go into the nearby town and have a "real" dinner. I guess they were tired of my gourmet cooking over the fire.

We met Cassie walking down the road. She was part of a bunch of firefighters that were training nearby, and her truck had broken down, so we gave her a ride into town. On the way, we got to talking about Bigfoot. She was a very serious gal, and here's the somewhat chilling story she told us.

I'm part of a crew of Hotshot firefighters. I work seasonally for the Forest Service, and I'm based in a small town in southwestern Oregon, although my crew will go wherever needed to fight fires. We're in top condition and often work in the hottest part of a fire, thus our name of Hotshots.

My crew has 20 total, mostly guys, though women are becoming more common. But it's hard work, and most people don't have what it takes. It requires mental as well as physical conditioning.

We're the elite of firefighting teams, along with the smokejumpers. People say we like to be in the wrong place at the wrong time. It's dangerous work.

So, I'll make this story short, as there really isn't that much to it, and you can choose to believe it or not. I don't care either way.

I've been ridiculed over it, so I've developed a bit of an attitude, and I usually don't even bother to tell it to anyone anymore.

There just happened to be a big fire in the Manti-La Sal Forest of southwestern Utah, and it had been whipped up by winds and hot dry conditions, so we got the call, as their resources had been stretched thin down there and it appeared that structures were being threatened. It was late in the season, September.

The fire was backing down one slope towards Interstate 15, and on the other front was burning towards Interstate 70, totally out of control. Picture a big square with I-15 on the left and I-70 on the top and you'll get the idea. It hadn't yet burned to where the two meet, and we didn't want that to happen.

The fire was about 30,000 acres at that point, and they were letting the interior burn out the thick overgrown vegetation that comes from fire suppression, which had been the norm for many years.

They were just trying to maintain the fronts from doing any more damage, but now that things were getting to the interstates, there was a real concern.

So, my crew, along with another Hotshot crew from Nevada, was staying in a spike camp, along with two engines, right along I-70, to monitor and contain the fire where it might jump the freeway.

The freeway had been closed because of the thick smoke and danger, and everyone wanted this fire to just back off so they could reopen it, so we were also doing some ground ignition, setting backfires.

The smoke was as thick as I've seen anywhere, and a hot wind was blowing in from the west. I was told the interior of the area had burned in a mosaic pattern, with some unburned areas that had been skipped over by the fire, and I think that would kind of explain where what saw came from. I'll get to that in a minute.

Anyway, my crew got the word that we needed to get further west along the freeway, as a new branch of the fire was coming up from the interior in that direction.

So we took off, and it was kind of weird to have the big four-lane freeway all to ourselves. We just tooled along on the eastbound lanes, going the wrong way, even though it was the right way for us.

We soon got to where we needed to be and got to work setting backfires. I could see a big column of smoke coming our way, and the wind was blowing straight towards us.

I was working along the northwest flank of the fire, when I sat down to take a break and drink some water. I was sitting on the guardrail, just sitting there, and that's when I saw them. It was just too bizarre, believe me.

The smoke was thick, and I was looking right into it, where the west wind was blowing it towards me, when I thought I could make out some figures.

I was surprised, because I was on the outer perimeter, and everyone else was to the east of me. I remember thinking at first that it was part of my crew, but then realizing it wasn't and wondering, "What the heck are people doing over there in the smoke?"

As I watched, a line of figures emerged from the smoke, walking slowly, like you would if you were in pain or feeling defeated. Maybe it was smoke inhalation, I don't know, but they were walking slow.

And as they emerged from the swirling smoke, I couldn't believe what I was seeing. These things weren't people at all.

At first I thought they were bears. We often see wildlife of all sorts fleeing from fires, but it soon became obvious they weren't bears.

They had faces that seemed human, what I could see through the smoke, but they were covered in dark hair, which hung from their arms. And they didn't seem to have any neck, it was like they were wearing hoodies, you know, jackets with the hoods up. And they were very muscular.

The line of figures was maybe fifty feet from me, and they acted like they didn't see me. There were seven of them, they looked like adults, all very large, maybe eight feet tall.

Then behind them came four smaller ones, like kids, various sizes, from about three feet to four or five feet tall.

At the very end was another very large adult. One of the adults seemed to be carrying something that looked like a young one.

They trudged to the guardrail and stepped over it like it wasn't even there, then crossed the freeway, the median, then the other side of the freeway, then disappeared into the forest.

Not one of them acknowledged me, even though I know they had to be able to see me.

I sat there for a long time, trying to figure out what I had seen, and then a chill went up my spine, and I thought I was going to throw up, just from tension.

Shortly thereafter, some of my crew came over to help me work the flank, so I grabbed my Pulaski and got back to work. I never said a word to anyone.

It was the most bizarre thing that's ever happened to me in my life, watching those ghost figures in the smoke.

[11] Hanging Around the Campfire

* *

Sitting around a campfire deep in the backcountry, a story like the following told by a fellow named Brian gives you the chills. This was one of those nights when we all just sat around the fire until we started nodding off, too scared to go to our tents.

This happened to me and some friends about five years ago, in a national park in Washington. The park has a backcountry permit system—you can't camp without a permit, and we had to apply for this way ahead of time.

We thought we'd see lots of people, as it's a popular park, but we saw almost no one the entire time we were there.

At the time, I worked for a high-tech company in Seattle. A group of us decided to go backpacking together. We were all pretty avid outdoorsmen, some were hikers and a couple of the guys were serious climbers. We were all seasoned and experienced outdoorsmen. There were seven of us, all told.

So, we finally got the permit and made our plans and were soon camped in a high alpine basin deep within the park. I'd rather not say exactly where this happened.

It took us a good hard day to get in there, carrying all that gear on our backs. We were tired, and after we set up camp, we built a fire and cooked dinner.

It was soon dark, as it had taken quite awhile to set everything up. We had a great spaghetti dinner and were soon all crashed out in our tents, exhausted.

I'll add that I was the only one with any kind of weapon. I had a large Bowie knife, and I slept with it under my pillow. I'd had a run-in with a black bear in Yellowstone and always carried that knife. The bear hadn't harmed me, just scared me trying to get into my tent, but I hadn't had any defense at all, so thus the knife on this trip. This was before you were allowed to carry guns in national parks.

I guessed it to be about 3 a.m. when I woke. I just lay there. Something had awakened me, but I didn't know what. Then I heard some scuffling noise and some low talking. I crawled out of my tent and found several of the guys up and talking in a whisper.

I didn't even have time to ask when I heard it. From way off in the distance, I mean several miles away, we could hear a sound that, for lack of better description, sounded like an air-raid siren. It was the weirdest thing you can imagine, being way up there in the wilderness, to hear a siren.

But what was even weirder, and what left me with a knot in the pit of my stomach, was the fact that the noise was moving, was gradually getting closer. And whatever was making it had lungs like a freight train, if a train had lungs. Whatever it was had a huge set of lungs, it sounded miles away and yet was so distinct. It really filled the air, it had vibrations to it.

By now the rest of the guys were up, and everyone looked concerned. It was a unique situation for all of us.

And remember, I was the only one armed, and not very well, at that. A Bowie knife isn't really much of a weapon in a deal like that.

We kind of ended up bunched together, and someone said we should build a fire. So we ended up grabbing some wood from the forest around us, and put it with the bit of wood from our earlier fire.

We built a fire, and some of the guys continued to gather wood, but no one would get far from camp. We used our headlamps, and it was kind of eerie seeing all the lights nervously moving around the forest while that noise just got closer and closer.

By the time it was near us, it actually shook the forest. It was the most intense sound I've ever heard, and it brought shivers to the back of my neck, literally.

Before long it was really close to our camp, and it was so loud it made my ears ring, you could actually feel the sound waves going through the air.

It was just this intense siren sound, it would go from low pitch to high and drop back down again. Everyone stood with their backs to the fire, and we all had big sticks, except for me, and I had my knife in my hand.

When the creature got to the edge of our camp, it just went crazy. It stopped making the siren sound and started with a high-pitched screaming, then it would stop and growl, then go back to the screaming.

That growl was absolutely terrifying, it was deep and throaty and mean sounding. We were all scared to death.

Nobody said a word. We all just stood there, white as ghosts. Once in awhile the fire would kind of die down and someone would grab some wood from the pile and get it going again. This seemed to enrage the creature, and it would start screaming again.

It then began circling our camp, and we could hear it breaking through the bushes and trees. It had to be large.

I swear, I was so scared I don't remember much except praying and standing there with that big knife held out in front of me.

The creature circled and circled. It knocked down several fairly large trees, a good eight inches in diameter, and one of those nearly fell on us.

We just continued to stand there in a pitiful circle around the fire. I worried that we would run out of wood, and sure enough, it was about 5 a.m., and the last bit of wood was burning.

I said to one of the guys that we needed a plan for when the wood ran out. The creature was still circling our camp. It had settled down some and wasn't screaming any more, but from the way it was breaking trees left and right, it still seemed very angry.

Once in awhile, it would lob a small tree at us—trees too green to burn, and you could see the roots. It had ripped them from the ground.

So, we made a plan, though it wasn't much of one. We hadn't had our headlights turned on, as we wanted to conserve the batteries. We decided that when the fire was dead, we'd all turn on our lights and shine it at wherever the creature was, and keep shining the lights until dawn.

We knew we could last because we all had fresh batteries, the trip having just started. If the creature wasn't afraid of our lights, well, who knows then?

So the fire died out, and we turned on our headlamps and shone them at the creature as it circled the camp. I was amazed at the energy it had, it hadn't slowed down at all.

This wasn't much of a plan, but it was all we had. If it tried to attack, we agreed to light some sticks on fire, we'd go down fighting. A kind of pitiful plan, really.

When we turned on our lights and shone them into the woods, the creature stopped short. We could now see a pair of glowing red eyes looking at us, and the eyes were a good eight feet off the ground. This scared the you-know-what out of me.

And the eyes had no flicker to them. We hadn't seen any red eyes before, it was like it had just turned them on at will.

It stood there, eyes glowing, just out of the circle of our lights, then just disappeared.

The quiet, the silence, its disappearance, were all really scary because we had no idea what was going on. Was it sneaking up on us? The uncertainty factor was really chilling.

If I tried to describe the fear of that night in detail, it would be a mixture of hopelessness, chilling terror, and astonishment.

Finally, I could see the first light of dawn as the sky to the east began to turn a pale blue. It was still a good hour before it was really light enough to see much, and by then we had all pretty much collapsed around the cold fire ring.

The night had taken its toll on us all, but not one of us went to sleep sitting there, we just sat in shock.

As soon as it was light enough to see, everyone got up and began breaking camp. There was no discussion about it, it just happened. Everyone was exhausted, but we put on our packs and headed back the way we'd come in.

It was only a few hours later when we got to the trailhead and our cars. Going downhill and pushed by fear, we got out really fast.

At that point, the sun was bright and the night seemed like a weird dream. We sat down on some rocks and began talking for the first time. I made some coffee, and someone else broke out some granola bars and cheese, and we ate like famished men, which we were.

No one had any idea what to make of any of this except one guy who had been raised in the Northwest, and he said he knew what it was. He said it was a Bigfoot, and a very angry one, probably because we had invaded its territory.

Would it have harmed us? Yes, he was sure of it, as angry as it was, it wasn't bluffing.

After a bit of talking about all this, we left and went to our respective homes. I don't think any of us have been back in the park since then. I know I've given up camping completely and have no desire to be out in the woods.

I still have an interest in the park and read the news about that area, and strangely enough, several hikers have disappeared in that part of the park since then.

A couple of years later, I took it upon myself to contact a park ranger and tell her of our experience that night.

She was very quiet, then told me what she was going to say was strictly off the record, but that the park service had quit issuing permits for that section of the park and knew something strange was afoot.

They weren't sure how to address the situation. Strange tracks had been found, and she, herself, had something black and huge stalk her while on horseback patrol not too far from where our camp had been.

She won't go into that area alone, and the park service has now prohibited anyone from going in there at all. She told me they've had two rangers transfer and a couple of seasonals quit, and she was trying to transfer also.

I told her I understood how she feels. I myself have no desire to ever go there again.

[12] A Dream Gone Bad

Cindie was a pilot who flew one of my wealthy flyfishing clients to meet me at the airport in Hayden, Colorado for a week-long guided expedition.

We invited her to our welcome dutch-oven dinner, and when we got to talking, she told one of the most unique and terrifying Sasquatch stories I've ever heard.

My name is Cindie, and I used to live in Fairbanks, Alaska. My husband (at the time, we're now divorced) always wanted a remote cabin in the Alaskan outback. It was a dream he'd had since before we met.

He was a highly-stressed oil executive, and I think this represented a sort of freedom to him, a return to his childhood days when he and his family lived near Lake Tahoe.

So he finally got to the position financially where he could make this dream come true, and he did.

He went and bought a parcel of land, and it was truly remote, you could only get in there with a bush plane, a float plane. This is not unusual in that part of Alaska.

I met my husband flying. I'm a bush pilot, so my job for the project was to get us in and out of there, along with supplies for this new undertaking, this cabin.

We had spent hours on the plans, but it was a modest cabin because we were limited by the supplies we could get in there.

We spent a lot of time camping on the site, it was by a large lake, and we'd walk around and picture this and that until we decided where we wanted the cabin.

But I should've known something serious was up when Del, my husband, decided suddenly to change the plans.

It had to be close enough that we could easily reach the plane, yet we wanted some trees around it for ambiance. But Del now changed his mind and wanted the cabin right by the lake, where we could easily reach the plane.

This happened after I had flown back into town to get more supplies, as we'd decided to stay an extra week, and when I came back, Del was acting weird.

He seemed nervous, and when I asked him about it, he said he'd seen what he thought was a grizzly, but there was something strange about it, it had walked on two feet.

Bears will sometimes do this, so we talked about it, and Del just couldn't seem to calm down, so we decided to leave. On the way out, he told me he wanted the cabin right next to the lake. I had no problem with that, but it was just the beginning.

We flew back in a week later, and Del spent some time walking around the area looking for tracks. He said he wanted to know if grizzlies had been around. He didn't find anything, but it seemed like he was still very nervous, always looking over his shoulder.

He didn't sleep well in the tent, in fact, he ended up trying to sleep in the plane. At that point, I told him we needed to reassess this whole thing. If he was that nervous about bears, maybe we should just drop the entire idea.

He seemed to come back around and get it together. He wanted that cabin, it was his childhood dream, and no bear was going to deny him that. So back to the plans, but he then decided he would make it a bear-proof cabin.

He redesigned it to be really strong, with big logs and a lot of reinforcement. We were going to have a logging crew come in and cut the logs on our own land for the cabin. This was not a quick project, as the logs would have to cure before we could even use them.

We had the logs cut, and the cabin looked to be substantial in thickness and construction, if not in size. It was then that Del announced we wouldn't have regular windows, as bears could knock out the glass and get in.

I agreed, but wasn't prepared for his new idea—the cabin would have windows like you'd see in old castles, sort of cross-shaped, like for a crossbow, and narrow, only a foot or so wide. We wouldn't have to carry as much glass in that way, he said, and nothing could get in.

The next change of plans was to add a second story with a deck, so he could see all around and enjoy the countryside without actually being away from the cabin. It was almost like being a prisoner, I thought, but didn't say anything.

At this point, I was beginning to think this whole idea was getting crazy. I had yet to see one grizzly there, but I knew they were around and could be dangerous. But why live somewhere you were scared all the time?

I told him we should maybe consider a cabin in Colorado or somewhere there weren't grizzlies, but he said we were already into this, and he'd see it through, plus he wanted a place close enough he could come on the weekends.

Colorado was too far. He had the money to have a cabin wherever he wanted, and this was the place.

It was finally the next spring, and construction began. I flew a couple of log-house builders in and supplied them. They had a big cabin tent to live in, and they figured it would easily take the two of them all summer to get the logs up.

Del and I would go out there on weekends and check up on them and resupply them. It was a truly beautiful spot, and it was beginning to be fun, watching the cabin take shape.

We'd camp on the weekends, and Del seemed much more relaxed with more people around. We'd sit by the campfire in the evenings and tell tales, roast marshmallows, swat mosquitoes, that sort of thing.

Finally, by mid-summer, the shell was taking shape and it was becoming more clear what the building would look like. I was starting to get excited, even though it wouldn't be until next summer that we could use it.

Del's attitude was completely changed also. He was now comfortable around the area and had apparently forgotten the bears, even though the workers had seen a couple in the distance.

They were, of course, well armed (the workers, not the bears). If you spend much time in the Alaska outback, you're going to see grizzlies, and you're wise to be armed.

Well, one day I got a call on my satellite phone. It was Joe, one of the construction guys out at the site. He said we needed to get out there ASAP. He wouldn't tell me why, just get the hell out here, he said, it was an emergency.

Del was gone, he was at a meeting in Washington, trying to work with a lobbyist about something to do with the oil business. I really didn't want to go out there alone, but it sounded urgent.

At this point I knew the guys really well, they were very credible and trustworthy, and Joe was not mincing words. But I called my buddy Simon and had him go out with me, he was a fellow bush pilot. I didn't know what I would find and might need help.

I knew something was wrong the minute we landed on the lake. I could see both of the guys on the shore, ready to go. They were carrying their rifles.

They waded out to the plane a bit, running, and I barely had time to shut the prop off before they were on board.

They both said to get the hell out now, as fast as we could. But I wanted to inspect the site and see what they'd done. They refused to get out of the plane and told me we had to go, it was a dangerous situation.

We needed to get the hell out of there right then and now. There was a real sense of urgency, so I took back off. They were fine, so it wasn't something medical.

I did decide to circle over the cabin site, and my eyes couldn't believe what I saw.

Half the building had been razed to the ground. I mean, it looked like a tornado had struck it. Logs were scattered around like matchsticks, and these were big heavy logs. The guys had used a makeshift crane to raise them.

And the rest of the building was being demolished as we flew above it.

As I flew in a circle, I could see several large dark brown creatures pushing down walls and tearing everything up. Their strength and fury was unbelievable, and as we flew over, they looked up, and we could see their faces.

These weren't bears at all. They looked human, except for their size and hair all over. They also looked enraged.

"Sasquatch," said Joe. "Now let's get the hell out of here, go back to Fairbanks. If we came back down, they'll kill us."

On the way back to Fairbanks, Joe and his partner, Larry, told a story of how they had at first heard sounds in the forest, at first distant, then closer and closer, like wood knocking on wood.

This went on for a couple of days, and the two had been so unnerved by it that they took turns on guard while the other slept.

They had been unable to work for fear and for a feeling of being watched. Remember, we're out in the Alaskan outback, one of the most remote places on earth.

Finally, the wood knocking had turned into vocalizations during the night. Joe swore he had heard what sounded like monkey chatter, and later, deep growls.

He described the growls as having a lot of volume, like something with a huge chest. He also heard what sounded like some kind of conversations, but he couldn't make out words. It was nonsensical to him, kind of like some Oriental language.

They were afraid of grizzlies, but grizzlies didn't play games with their prey like these animals seemed to be doing, which made them much scarier.

Next, the growls turned into rocks being thrown. The two had made it through the night, terrified, rocks landing on their tent roof and causing it to sag, but by daylight things had quieted down. They were feeling braver and decided to investigate.

That's when they found the footprints and knew exactly what they were dealing with—Sasquatch. Now they were even more terrified. They tried to call me to come get them out, but they couldn't get through, even with a sat phone.

They spent the entire day trying to call while gathering discarded log ends for a fire. The Sasquatch seemed to be sleeping, as there was no activity during the day.

The next night was spent in true fear—fear they would never get out alive and fear that comes from hearing huge logs being thrown through the air. The Sasquatch were destroying the cabin.

A couple of times they could hear something near their tent, and they would shoot their rifles, and it would then retreat back into the night. They had decided not to actually shoot at anything, as the last thing they needed was an enraged wounded Sasquatch and friends enacting revenge.

No telling if their rifles would even make a dent in something that big, an animal big enough to throw logs around. They kept a big bonfire burning all night right outside their tent.

By morning, they had been able to get a signal and called me. The Sasquatch hadn't seemed to notice them as the two went to the edge of the lake, where they hid behind rocks, rifles ready, waiting until they saw me come in.

They had been afraid the Sasquatch would swim out to the plane and try to wreck it, which they could have easily done, so they were relieved when they got on board and we took off.

When we got back to Fairbanks and landed, they both quit on the spot, and I paid them. I also reimbursed them for the cabin tent they'd left behind.

I figured Del and I could go back out and get all the gear. I had no idea how he would take this, but I knew it would mean the end of the project.

When Del got back, I told him about what had happened and he seemed obsessed with talking to Joe and Larry, which he did.

He then told me he'd seen a Sasquatch on day one, that's why he'd been so nervous, but he hadn't trusted his eyes. Now, he refused to go back out to the site.

I was also scared, I had actually seen the Sasquatch and the power they had, but I really wanted to go get our gear. We had left some nice equipment out there.

But I couldn't find anyone who would go with me. Even my pilot friend Simon refused and tried to talk me out of going.

So, I decided to go alone. Maybe it was stupid, but I somehow felt that the Sas had probably already destroyed everything and left, it was now two weeks later. And I could circle around and check it out, see if I spotted anything before landing.

I was born and raised in Alaska, and I have a sort of determination that comes from having to make do. I wanted the nice tools that had been left out there, plus the camping gear. It was expensive stuff.

Del was beside himself. He threatened to divorce me if I went. My feelings were that he should at least have come with me to offer protection while I collected the gear, but he wouldn't do it. In retrospect, he was the smarter of the two of us in this case.

Like I said, we soon divorced, but it really had little to do with that, it had more to do with differing world views and incompatibilities. Ironically, he now lives in a cabin in Colorado.

I took my bear rifle with me, and also a handgun. When I got there, I circled several times, looking for bears or Sasquatch. At that point, I was scared to death, but I decided to go through with it, I'd flown clear out there.

The cabin was totally destroyed, nothing stood, just logs strewn around. I looked for the tent, it was gone, then I saw what looked to be shreds of it all over.

This was bad, but maybe I could at least get a few of the tools and such. They'd been using a Brunton level I really wanted, it had belonged to my dad and had sentimental value. I landed on the lake.

The Sasquatch must have heard me coming, although I didn't know it. I got out of the plane and anchored it, then jumped onshore. I would work quickly, get the level first, be on guard, get out fast.

It suddenly dawned on me that I was taking my life into my hands foolishly, just for an old level, and my dad would not have been happy about that. But I continued, kind of compelled, actually.

I went to the campsite and sure enough, the tent was completely gone, but shreds of canvas were here and there. I had my digital camera, and I took photos.

There was literally nothing there to retrieve, everything was gone. The guys had left their personal stuff, clothes, cookset, etc., and nothing was there. The Sas had taken it, apparently.

I was on guard, watching as I went, half scared to death. I then went to the cabin site, looking for the level and some of the expensive tools. Nothing.

I couldn't find anything worth retrieving, but the photos were worth the trip, I decided. Del wouldn't believe it.

I suddenly saw something reflecting in the sun. It was my dad's level, half buried under debris. This was a hand level, a very nice old-fashioned one, and I was very happy to have it back.

But now, just as suddenly as I'd spotted the level, I felt an indescribable and sudden urge to get back on the plane, a fight or flight feeling. I was being watched. The hair on my neck stood up.

I drew my handgun. I'd left the rifle in the plane, as it was too bulky to carry while trying to collect stuff. I slowly turned in a circle, assaying the situation.

I saw nothing, but I somehow knew they were there. I felt foolish, terrified, stupid to have come back.

I now began walking back to the plane, constantly looking around me. There were trees and big rocks everywhere. Each could have a Sasquatch behind it, and I had to cut through a part of the forest to get to the plane, as a small shore cliff prevented me from taking a straight path.

Why had I come back? Would anyone ever find me?

Now I could hear them coming. I could hear wood-knocking in the trees to my left, then to my right, very close.

I wanted to run, but instinct said not to, to not show fear. I carefully made my way through a group of large boulders, then entered the small grove of trees I had to cut through to get back.

I could hear footsteps. I was being followed, and close. I could turn and face them and shoot or keep going and try to get back quickly before they decided to attack, if they were going to. I decided to just keep going.

I've read a lot about Bigfoot since then, and I've read they aren't as territorial around women as men. Maybe they decided I wasn't a threat, because they never showed their faces. I did hear some monkey chatter, or what sounded like it.

I was soon on the plane and out of there. I never felt so happy in my life to be off that lake.

What really freaked me out was when I got back and downloaded the photos on my computer. Del was looking at them, he just couldn't believe the destruction, but after awhile, he got even more interested and started zooming in on things.

Every single picture I took had at least one set of eyes in it, eyes that glowed red, eyes in the trees in the background. And these guys were huge, at least seven or eight feet off the ground. Every single one of them.

Del figured, based on the number of photos I took, that there were at least six or seven Sasquatch right there when I was wandering around.

That still gives me the chills.

After we divorced, I took a job at a flight school as an instructor as far from the Alaskan outback as I could get, in Tucson, Arizona.

[13] BASE Jumpers

I met Bodie one day while out fishing alone, which is what we flyfishing guides do on our day off. Bodie was a very likable young guy who was out mountain biking with his girlfriend.

He had recently moved to the Colorado mountains from northern California and was wanting to learn how to flyfish, so I invited him to come on one of my guided tours at no charge.

He made himself my helper and more than earned his keep, along with telling this story that was the highlight of the campfire tales for that whole trip.

I'm a base jumper. You know, BASE, the four categories of fixed objects from which one can jump—Buildings, Antennae, Spans (bridges), and Earth (cliffs). My preference is the latter, cliffs, although I once jumped off the LDS building in Salt Lake City.

It's hard to describe, and it's more than just the jump, it also involves the climbing to get there, seeing the awesome scenery, and then the actual feeling of floating like a bird.

It's not like I have kids or a family or anything, and it's actually not as dangerous as people make it out to be.

Usually, anyway.

But I want to tell you about an experience that turned a normally calm and predictable jump into a nightmare. I'm still not sure what actually happened, and I'm at even more of a loss as to why it happened.

My jump buddy is a close friend named Teller, we've been buds since college. Teller and I started out snowboarding together while in school, and then that sort of evolved into extreme boarding, then into BASE jumping, 'cause we could do that year round, which we couldn't do with the snowboarding.

We'd been jumping together for about two years when this happened. I mean, we were seasoned jumpers and knew what we were doing.

The only problem we'd ever had was when I underestimated the height of a bridge over a canyon once and nearly hit the ground before my chute opened. I learned not to trust my judgement, but to actually verify heights, 'cause you need room for your chute to open. That was a close call, for sure.

Well, so was this incident. Teller and I really liked jumping from some huge cliffs near Yosemite National Park. We're not actually in the park, so they can't restrict what we do, but it's beautiful big granite walls like in the park, just stunning.

The cliffs are accessed by driving up into the mountains, then we park and have to hike a couple of miles to get to the top of this one mountain, which has one entire side that's a beautiful vertical high cliff, over 1500 feet high.

You land in a meadow and can just walk up the highway to get back to your car. Way easier than some of the places we jump, so the fun-to-work ratio is very good. We had lots of fun jumping these cliffs, since at that time we both lived only a couple of hours away.

Anyway, it was a beautiful summer day, and we had decided to go for it. We were in good spirits and had nearly reached the summit of the mountain, when we kept thinking someone was behind us.

We never saw anyone up there before, it was way off the beaten path, though the road was nearby. There was just no reason for anyone to go there. There was lots of scenery around, nobody would walk up this huge hill for much of anything, except to jump, and we hadn't told anyone about it, it was kind of our own secret place.

So, we kept hearing noises, like someone was either behind us, or nearby in the trees. Teller was kind of afraid it was a bear, so we kept hoofing it, we were actually almost jogging. But it was too steep for that, so we'd have to pull back into a walk after awhile, then we'd hear it again.

It sounded like something big walking through the brush, kind of breaking twigs and all that, and we could sometimes hear a loud breathing sound. We really didn't know what to make of it.

After awhile, it was getting kind of eerie, and Teller said maybe we should turn around and go back. But at that point, I told him, we were closer to the cliffs than the car, and whatever it was could no way follow us off the cliffs.

So we kept moving forward, and this thing kept moving with us. And as we went along, it seemed less inclined to hide itself.

We were now catching glimpses of something that looked very large and that was all brown, from head to toe, and that wasn't really that far off to the side of us.

Teller was convinced it was a bear, and I wasn't convinced it wasn't, but it seemed eerie for a bear. Bears don't normally behave like that, stalking people.

But we were both convinced it was a bear because there was no way it could be anything else. It certainly wasn't a human.

I found out later that Teller knew exactly what it was, he told me that himself. He just hadn't wanted to totally freak me out.

We were soon getting really spooked by this. We had done this jump a good half-dozen times and never had anything like this happen.

We just kept jogging to the top, trying to keep a good pace up, and this thing just stayed right with us. In hindsight, I think Teller was right, we should've gone back to the car.

At the top of the mountain, there's a clearing and no trees, and this is where we usually regrouped and caught our breath, ate a snack, put on our chutes, that kind of thing.

Well, we got to the clearing, which was about a hundred feet from the edge, and neither of us wanted to stop, but we had to, to put on our chutes.

So we both got our chutes on muy rapido, and I worried a bit that our fears might be compromising our safety, as we normally did full safety checks of everything.

I told Teller, we need to slow down and check everything out, we can't afford any mistakes, bear or no bear.

I checked out my gear carefully, but Teller didn't, he just stood there looking back into the forest, saying he could hear it, and it was coming closer.

Let me add some pertinent information here, something I had forgotten until we were actually standing on that mountain hearing this thing coming through the woods.

The last couple of times we'd been up there, we'd found some weird tracks, and Teller had said they were Bigfoot tracks. These things were a good six inches longer than my boot tracks, and several inches wider, and the toes were very clear.

There is no way they were bear tracks, but I'd told Teller that's what they were. I didn't want to lose my jump buddy, 'cause I knew he believed in Bigfoot, and I didn't. In fact, he claimed to have seen one once when he was a kid, but I just figured he had an overactive imagination.

But now I was scared, too, because I could hear this thing making a noise that's hard to describe, but sounded like something big beating on its chest. Yeah, I know, right out of Tarzan or something, but that's what it sounded like.

Teller just stood there. I think he was having a flashback or something. I turned and grabbed his shoulders and said, "Let's go, man, let's jump, it's time to go."

He turned back to me like he'd forgotten who he was and where he was, a look of puzzlement on his face.

"Teller!" I was almost yelling at him, right in his face, "Now! Let's go!"

I grabbed his arm and started pulling him along. And then he got it and started with me towards this rock promontory that we normally jumped from.

Then he stopped and turned around, and so did I.

God almighty, what a terrifying sight! This thing was only a few hundred feet from us and was now rushing towards us at full speed. It was huge, bigger than a Kodiak Bear I once saw in Alaska, and it was on its hind legs. And terribly fast.

"Oh God! Run, run, run!" I screamed at Teller and madly ran for the rock. He was right behind me. We were both running as fast as we could, and this thing was catching up.

I reached the rock and didn't even stop, I just bailed off the edge, assuming Teller was right behind me.

It seemed to take forever to float down, and I looked above me and saw no signs of Teller. This worried me beyond words.

I don't even remember landing and picking up my chute or anything, all I recall is looking up for Teller for the longest time.

No Teller.

I sat on the ground and started to cry, in relief that I'd made it and in fear that he hadn't.

I have no idea how long I sat there, waiting for him to come down, but probably only 10 minutes, though it seemed like an hour or two.

Then I panicked. I had to get back up there and see what had happened, but not by myself. At that point, I stashed my chute behind a tree and ran for the highway.

I did stop on the way and dialed 911 and managed to get out that we needed search and rescue out here and gave my location. Thank God I had a cell signal, often I didn't in the backcountry.

I flagged down a car. It was a couple of hikers, and they dropped me off at my car on up the road. There, I again called 911 and was assured a SAR team was on its way.

I didn't dare go up there alone. I knew it would mean the end. No need in us both dying, but I admit I felt like a true coward, and if I'd had a gun, I would've gone and looked for Teller. He was my best friend. But I couldn't face that beast alone unarmed.

It was a good half-hour or so later when a couple of SAR vehicles pulled up. I didn't have the heart to tell them the whole story, they would think I was nuts and maybe call off the search, so I just told them my buddy hadn't jumped with me and must be hurt up there.

There were six guys, so I figured there would be safety in numbers. Off we went up the mountain. I'm in good shape, but it seemed like we were climbing Everest. I was so tired, I just wanted to be home, safe. With Teller.

I was very apprehensive and stayed in the middle of the group, keeping an eye out for anything that could be the Bigfoot, but I saw and heard nothing.

We finally got to the top, and I was dreading what I would see, and sure enough right at the rock outcropping was Teller, just lying there, quiet and still.

I couldn't bear to go over there, but the SAR guys did. I finally got up the courage and walked over to where he lay.

His chute was ripped off him and torn to shreds. It looked like someone had cut it up with scissors. But he had no marks on him, no blood, nothing.

One of the guys, a paramedic, said Teller had a good heartbeat. He seemed to be unconscious. One of the SAR guys was radioing for a helicopter carry out.

While they were doing all this, I sat by him for awhile, talking to him, until I saw his eyelids flutter a bit, then open. He was awake!

He seemed really disoriented, and the medic wouldn't let him sit up, and rigged up some kind of saline solution or something into his veins.

Finally, Teller started talking to me, and all he could say was, "Is it gone? Is it gone?"

I assured him all was fine. They were going to helicopter him to the hospital, and he'd be fine. He actually grabbed onto my arm and wouldn't let me go. But when the helicopter came, they made him let loose, as I couldn't ride with him.

I told him I'd see him soon in the hospital and to be well, and he responded with, "Don't walk back down alone, Bodie, don't. Promise me you won't." I didn't have to promise him, there was no way I would have.

Seeing the chopper come into that clearing and the finesse of the pilot was something else. Teller was soon gone, and we all started back down the mountain.

Some of the guys started asking me what I thought had happened, especially with the shredded chute. It looked too weird.

I didn't want to talk about it until we got back to the vehicles, but once we were back, I told them the whole story. I didn't think they would believe me, and they pretty much looked incredulous.

But when I was done, one of the guys pulled a little digital camera from his pocket and passed it around, telling everyone to check out the photos he'd taken up there.

He was the one who kept track of everything and did the follow-up reports. The camera made its rounds, with a few comments like holy sheet and damnation. And everyone was quiet when I looked at the pictures, watching my face.

The camera had photos of Teller lying there, of his shredded chute, of the helicopter and all that. But towards the end, there were a number of photos of huge tracks, Bigfoot tracks, and the guy had put his own boot next to them for size. They were huge.

I was vindicated.

Teller was fine, although he stayed in the hospital for three days for treatment of a concussion.

He later told me he'd been almost to the edge when the Bigfoot had reached him and grabbed him by the chute, ripping it off. There was no way he could now jump, and he was terrified, so he just turned and stood his ground.

He watched as the creature shredded the chute, almost as if he knew what it was for. He said the Bigfoot then turned and walked to the edge where I'd jumped and apparently watched as I floated down.

It then started coming towards Teller, but for some reason he was now calm and knew somehow that it didn't mean him any harm. It instead seemed puzzled and curious.

It just stood and looked at him, its eyes huge and inquisitive. The two of them just stood looking at each other when Teller turned a bit, caught his toe on a rock and fell, hitting his head and blacking out.

Teller was able to laugh a bit, saying he had nearly crossed the barrier between man and Bigfoot until he stupidly crashed and burned.

I got the SAR guy to send us copies of the photos. The very last one he'd taken was of a dead crow that had been placed next to Teller's head. For some reason, that really freaked me out. I would never go up on that mountain again.

But Teller says he thinks the Bigfoot was trying to stop us from jumping, thinking we would harm ourselves, and maybe it felt bad and left the bird in case he woke up and was hungry. Teller says he's going to go back up there someday and leave a big bag of beef jerky, but I bet and hope he doesn't.

[14] House Arrest

· ·

I once guided a group of women from Montana, which was quite a trip. We had a blast, and they caught some big fish. We had some great campfire talks, and this is one of the more memorable stories from that trip.

My name is Carolyn, and my husband, Ed, and myself had a very scary, terrifying experience I'd like to relate. I hope this isn't too long, but I need to first give you some background.

My husband grew up on a wheat farm in North Dakota. I'm from Arizona. We met while in school, and we both ended up working for the state government in Arizona and living there our entire working careers, having a son.

But when we retired, Ed wanted to do something different, and he saw a wheat farm for lease in Montana, so we leased it and moved up there.

I know, we kind of had things backwards, moving to snow country when we retired. Most people do it the other way around, moving to Arizona.

We moved about ten miles north of Bozeman, Montana, to a farm right at the foot of the Bridger Mountains. It was a beautiful place, right where a small stream comes out of a small canyon. Sometimes, after we first got there, we'd walk up that stream and have picnics.

Of course, we knew winters would be harder than we were used to, but Bozeman was nearby, and with the university there, it seemed like there was always something going on, concerts, lectures, that kind of thing, so I knew I wouldn't have any problem finding things to do. And the shopping was really good, several nice grocery stores.

The farm wasn't really big by wheat farm standards, only 200 acres, but it was plenty for us. After all, this was just for Ed, so he could go back to his roots and not go nuts, being retired. I tend to have more interests than he does, I'm more of a hobbyist. I do watercolor painting and all sorts of things.

The farm came with all the necessary equipment, everything needed to farm. The old guy wanted to retire, he was in his 80s. He wanted to sell it, so we agreed if that happened, we'd move on.

We'd enjoy the experience while we could. We were retired and could always go elsewhere. We weren't interested in buying it.

Ed was in seventh heaven after we moved there. He tinkered with equipment and did some handyman work on the old barn.

We lived in the old farmhouse, which had only two bedrooms, both upstairs. It was cozy and homey and had space for a big garden.

Since it was spring, we needed to get on things right away. Ed had to get the fields ready and plant the wheat. It was dryland farming, so the weather was our make it or break it variable.

We bought the seed and provided the diesel fuel and work, and we would split the profit with the landlord—that was the deal, our rent was included. I don't know how that stacks up with most sharecropper deals, but we were happy with it.

Fast forward to mid-summer. I had a beautiful garden going and had painted the interior of the house, making it bright and cheerful, as the old guy hadn't touched it for years.

The farm was a wonderful place. I'd go out and do watercolors of the big cottonwoods around the house with the redwing blackbirds singing in them.

It was so quiet there, so peaceful, and I really enjoyed going into town some and had made a few friends in the artist community—we'd go downtown and sit in the little espresso cafes. I was loving life in Montana. Of course, we hadn't been through a winter yet.

It was early July when I got the call from Gary, our son. It changed everything. He and his wife were getting divorced.

It was her idea, she had met another guy and had already moved in with him. Gary was devastated, he had no idea anything was wrong.

But what really choked him up was the way she just abandoned their little girl, Ellie. She told Gary he could have custody, she had never wanted kids anyway.

This was just a horrible thing to do, and Ellie was being really impacted by it, even though she was only four. Gary had a good attorney and was working on it.

This made us heartsick, but there was nothing we could do about it. But things soon got worse.

Gary had proceeded with the divorce, and it was almost final when he got word he'd lost his job. He was working for a defense contractor in Phoenix and their government contract had ended and wasn't being renewed.

Gary did electronics, so he hoped he could get another job soon. The poor guy was really having a hard time.

All of this is relevant to the story, so bear with me. This was the catalyst for everything that came after.

Ed and I decided we needed to help Gary out, so we offered to take Ellie, to have her come stay with us for the rest of the summer, or until Gary could get things straightened out.

To make a long story short, by August first, Ellie had come to live with us. We fixed up the second bedroom for her, and I tried to make it as cozy as possible.

Bozeman has some good second-hand shops, so I found everything I needed pretty cheap. And Ed fixed up a really cool old tire swing for her off one of the big trees.

Gary didn't tell her she would never see her home again, as he was also losing his house. We just tried to make it out to be a short stay with grams and gramps. This poor little girl had already been through the mill.

Let me tell you, there's a reason young people have kids, it's because they wear you out if you're not young.

Ellie was a little fireball of energy, but she was a real delight to have around.

She loved the farm and was soon exploring everything and seemed to be happy. She especially liked the swing, and would yell with delight when I pushed her in it.

I took her into town one day and bought her a little stuffed puppy, as she was missing their Beagle, Sparky.

That stuffed puppy never left her side. She carried it everywhere she went, even into the bathtub! I soon came to wonder how we'd lived without Ellie, she was such a treasure.

Then one night things changed. It was around three a.m., and Ellie came into our bedroom and woke me up, crying and scared. She said she saw a big monster face in her window.

All I could get out of her was that some big monster had been watching her through her window and woke her up. I tried to reassure her that she'd been having a bad dream, and I let her crawl into bed with us, stuffed puppy and all.

The next morning, she refused to go into her room, but I convinced her to come look out the window. I talked to her a long time, showing her how it would be impossible for anything to look through the window, as it was just too far off the ground.

This was the second story of the house, after all, and a good 15 feet to the window from the ground.

She seemed to be OK, and even spent the afternoon playing in her room and taking a nap. But when night came, she cried when I tried to put her to bed.

I decided maybe the entire affair of being in a strange house and missing her parents was causing nightmares, so I decided to sleep with her for awhile until she settled down.

With me in there, she seemed OK and finally went to sleep. After awhile, I got up and went to our bedroom and went to bed.

This time, it was about four a.m., and Ellie woke me up screaming. I ran quickly into her room. Ed also jumped up, and while I was comforting Ellie, he was outside with his big searchlight, looking around the house.

He found nothing, and we eventually all settled down, Ellie again sleeping with us.

That morning, I ended up sleeping in a bit, as I was tired, and when I got up, Ellie was still asleep. I went downstairs into the kitchen, where Ed was drinking coffee.

He looked upset and took me outside, where he showed me some very large tracks in the soft dirt out by the barn.

They were huge and had toes just like a human's, except two large men's feet would fit into one track. I was shocked, to say the least. Maybe Ellie hadn't been dreaming.

I got my camera and took photos, checked on Ellie, who was still asleep, and went back outside, where Ed was trying to find more tracks, but with no luck. The house was surrounded by lawn, and he didn't find anything anywhere else in the immediate area.

I'll never forget us both sitting around the little kitchen table, trying to figure out what was going on and what to do. It was just such a weird thing.

Our little farm now had an aura of strangeness to it, everything looked different. Ed said I should put curtains up in all the windows and not go outside after dark.

We spent that afternoon in town, buying curtains and getting groceries and taking Ellie to the park as a diversion. I actually didn't want to go back to the farm that evening, and I could tell Ed was thinking hard about the whole thing. He was just so pragmatic, and this didn't fit into anything either of us could explain.

I was busy the rest of the evening putting up the curtains, and Ed installed deadbolts on the outside doors. He had also purchased two motion sensor lights, and he installed those.

Ellie wanted to play on the swing, so he kept an eye on her while he was doing all this. No more letting her be alone outside in the yard. Everything was different.

With the curtains up over the windows, Ellie once again slept in her own room and seemed to be fine, as long as I would lie down with her until she was asleep.

Things got back to normal, but Ed and I were very cautious outside, especially after he discovered new tracks out in one of the wheat fields.

Ellie was never left alone, inside or out. I started thinking about moving, but I said nothing to Ed.

At the very least, we had to wait until the wheat harvest before doing anything. We didn't want to lose our investment and hard work.

Then one night, Ellie came into our room saying something was scratching on the walls. I told her it was just mice, but she slept with us again.

Ed went downstairs and was afraid to go outside, as he said one of the motion lights was on. He looked out through the windows and thought he may have seen something moving, but wasn't sure.

He ended up sitting downstairs all night with the lights off and a rifle in his hands, just in case. And sure enough, he found more tracks the next day.

We were both getting really spooked by this, and Ed decided to call the landlord.

The landlord was a really nice guy, a real character, and we both liked him, but that conversation got nowhere, and Ed was a bit put off that the old guy had actually laughed at him. So, I decided to call him myself.

He was very cordial and apologized for laughing at Ed, and then added that he'd been thinking about it and was wondering if it didn't have something to do with the canyon being called Devil's Canyon when he was a kid. Of course, no one had called it that for years, and he'd forgotten all about it until now.

He'd never had any problems like that, and he had no suggestions except to maybe get a big yard light. He said he'd pay for it out of his share of the harvest if Ed wanted to put one in.

Ed decided that would be a good idea and hired it done, as he had no way to install a pole by himself. Within a week we had a big halogen light that was on all night, lighting up the yard and even the barn area. We could see all around the house for a good ways. It definitely made me feel more secure.

I will never forget standing on the porch of that little farm house the first night we had that light and hearing a wailing sound in the distance. It was just the most eerie and strange and frightening sound you could ever hear, kind of like a combination of a coyote and a loon and a siren. It made the hair on the back of my neck stand up, and I went and got Ed.

He stood there, listening for awhile, then asked me if I wanted to leave. I said not until the harvest was done. He said we could rent something in town and he could commute to the farm, but I told him we really couldn't afford to have two places, and I didn't want him out here alone.

So we stayed. Harvest was only a couple of weeks or so away, surely we could wait it out. But I sure didn't sleep any that night.

One day, not long after, I got a call from Gary. His house was being foreclosed on, and he had nowhere to go. Could he come to the farm and help out until he could find work?

I said of course, it would be nice to have him, and Ellie would certainly be happy about seeing him and Sparky.

Ed was also happy, he could use the help at harvest, and he enjoyed being around him. Gary had such a good sense of humor and was very considerate.

That same afternoon, I had Ellie out in the yard and was swinging her on that big tire swing. I told her that her daddy was coming, and she was just so happy, she was giggling and laughing and yelling every time I'd swing her up high. She had her little stuffed puppy, holding it close to her chest.

But all of a sudden Ed came driving up on his tractor and jumped off, ran over to us yelling to get into the house. He followed us in and locked the doors and got out his rifle.

He said he'd seen something very large and dark watching us from the scrub oak thicket up the hill and it wasn't a bear, it was standing on two legs. He said it had to be a good nine feet tall.

Of course, we didn't let Ellie hear this. We were both scared stiff. We didn't go back outside at all that day. But nothing happened that night.

Gary arrived two days later from Phoenix. He'd driven all night and was exhausted. It's a good three-day trip down there, and he'd done it in two.

I gave him some dinner and then put him in Ellie's room on a spare rollaway bed. Now she'd have her dad there to keep her safe. She was a very happy little girl.

I hadn't had a chance to tell him about the weird events, I'd let him catch up on his sleep first.

Gary had brought their little Beagle, Sparky, with him. He was sure a cute little fellow, all black and tan and white. About all he did when he wasn't sleeping was sniff around and wag his tail—and beg for food.

The yard was fenced, which was good, because Beagles are notorious for hunting, following their noses and getting lost. The next day, Gary fixed up a little dog door so Sparky could go out into the yard whenever he wanted.

But Sparky wasn't out in the yard more than five minutes when he set up a howling like you've never heard, then ran into the door and squeezed under the TV stand, his ruff all up and his ears back and a look of sheer terror in his eyes.

Gary was puzzled, he'd never seen the little dog act like that. I looked all around outside, but saw nothing. I decided it was a good time to tell him what was going on.

Gary's reaction was at first to just laugh, but when he saw I wasn't kidding, and when he couldn't get Sparky out from under the stand, he started looking serious.

We talked some more, and I showed him photos of the footprints. He began to wonder if we shouldn't leave.

I told him I personally had a theory that the thing was attracted to Ellie and that we should never under any circumstances leave her alone for a second. It hadn't started coming around until Ellie showed up.

That's when my son told me he was going to see us through the harvest, but until then, he was going to be seriously job hunting in Bozeman. When he found something, we were all moving. He would do whatever we needed done to get out of there.

He later told Ed the same thing, and Ed agreed it might be a good thing to do. He was getting pretty spooked himself.

He'd actually talked to the neighbors, and they said they had seen this thing a couple of times up on the hills above our farm.

The days went quickly by, and Gary was gone quite a bit. Sometimes, we would hear that strange eerie call in the evenings. Sparky would run inside and hide under the bed, and sometimes it was all I could do to get him to even go outside during the day.

Gary started taking him into town with him on his job hunts, just to give the little dog a break.

It was nearly harvest time when Ed came into the house one day, white as a sheet. Gary and Sparky were gone, so it was just the three of us.

Apparently this creature had come up by his tractor while he was out clearing some weeds and had actually ran alongside him as Ed drove back to the house as fast as he could.

The creature hadn't tried to harm Ed, which it could've easily done, but it had scared him nearly to death.

He tried to describe it. It sounded like it was something half-human and half-ape, and very large with powerful and dangerous-looking shoulders, not much of a neck, and a large head, its body all covered with brown hair. He said its eyes looked very cunning.

And it was a female, as it had breasts. This made me even more concerned for Ellie, as it seemed interested in her. Maybe it had lost its own child. Who knows?

From then on, Ed carried his rifle with him. This left us unarmed at the house, so Gary brought home another rifle and some M80s he'd gotten from the game and fish department for scaring off deer.

He had finally found a job and was to start as soon as the wheat harvest was over. He would be working for a communications company.

He told us he was now looking for a house for us all and wanted us off that farm as soon as he and Ed harvested the wheat. They would start the next day.

That night, the howling was close by, and it started as soon as the sun set and went on for several hours. Ed finally went out on the porch and shot off several rounds with his rifle, which made it stop.

We then got a phone call from the neighbors, asking if everything was all right. They had also heard the howling and then the shots. They were beginning to be scared themselves, even though it had never bothered their place.

I think this was the beginning of the end, Ed shooting, even though he wasn't shooting at the creature. This somehow made things escalate, and Gary said Ed had made the thing angry.

Later that night, Gary and Ellie came into our room, saying they had heard something scratching at the walls like it was trying to get in. We then heard it scratching at our bedroom walls, as if it knew everyone was in there.

It then began banging on the walls so hard it made the house shake. And then it was on the roof, we could hear it walking around. That was how it had looked through Ellie's window, from the roof!

Gary started yelling at it, and it stopped. Of course, Sparky was hiding under the bed. Ellie was so scared she was sobbing, and I took her into the bathroom, where you couldn't hear much and it felt more secure.

She stopped crying, and I managed to divert her by telling her some bedtime stories, all the while trying to hear what was going on.

I suddenly heard several loud booms, then Ed came to the door and said it was OK to come out, they had lobbed some M80s and run it off. Gary would sit downstairs and watch for the rest of the night.

They had decided this would be our last night here. We'd go into town tomorrow and the two of them would commute to finish the harvest.

Ellie slept again with us while Gary dozed on the couch downstairs, armed with his rifle. Sparky also slept with us, under the covers next to Ellie and her little stuffed puppy.

I got up early and got the guys breakfast. Gary was half-asleep, but they would start the harvest, Ed driving the combine and Gary behind him, driving the wheat truck. Hopefully they could be done within a few days.

I started packing our stuff. We would leave in the evening, after the guys were done for the day. I had all day to pack, which seemed like lots of time, as we hadn't really brought that much stuff with us.

Ellie finally got up and I made her breakfast while Sparky ate his kibbles. Even the little dog looked tired.

I can see in retrospect how naive we all were. We should have left immediately. I started packing Ellie's room, putting her clothes and toys into a few boxes.

We would come get the furniture later, after we rented a place. We'd stay in a motel for a few days. The guys would harvest while I house hunted and took care of Ellie and Sparky.

After finishing Ellie's room, we hauled everything downstairs. Ellie was now interested in her box of toys, as we'd found a few things she'd forgotten she had, so I left her and Sparky in the kitchen for a bit while I packed my and Ed's things upstairs.

I have no idea what I was thinking. I actually wasn't thinking. I was tired and just trying to get things done, I guess. Big mistake.

The next thing I remember was hearing Sparky barking his head off. Beagles have loud barks, and his would turn into a bay, and it carried a long ways.

I instantly started down the stairs, and I wasn't half down them when I heard Ellie screaming.

Now Sparky was growling and it sounded like he was tearing into someone. Oh God, I can't tell you how scared I was.

I came running into the kitchen to total mayhem. This huge hairy monster had Ellie by the arm and was trying to drag her out the door, but Sparky was blocking its way.

Ellie was screaming in terror, and I began screaming, too, but in anger and fear all mixed together.

I picked up the nearest object, which was the cutting board, and I threw it as hard as I could at this creature, hitting it square in the head.

It dropped Ellie and started after me, but just then Sparky grabbed it by the calf and bit hard. The creature started screaming, and it made the whole house shake.

I was now trying to grab Ellie, and I managed to get her arm and drag her into the living room, terrified at the same time that Sparky would be killed.

I forgot all about the rifle sitting in the corner. I really didn't know how to use it, anyway.

I carried Ellie out the front door and to the car, but I didn't have the car keys! Just then, I saw Ed and Gary come driving up in the grain truck.

They saw us, and Gary grabbed Ellie and shoved us both into the cab of the truck. Just then, this creature came running out the kitchen door with Sparky close behind, the dog growling and snarling and the Bigfoot howling in anger and pain.

It was looking for Ellie, and when it saw us in the truck, it started our way.

That's when Ed started shooting at it. He hit it square on, and it reeled back a bit and fell to the ground.

Ed grabbed Sparky and yelled "Get in the truck," and he and Gary both jumped in and we took off.

I could see the creature getting up. It might be wounded, but it was coming after us, and it was fast!

I've never seen Ed drive like that, he had that old truck really spun up and we were out of there! I could see the creature trying to catch us, but Gary shot out the window at it, and it seemed to reconsider and stop.

I know he didn't hit it. All we had were .22 rifles, and after seeing how big that thing was, I don't think Ed's bullet made a dent.

The next couple of days are a blur, I hardly remember anything, except hiding in our motel room and trying to calm myself and Ellie and also taking Sparky to the vet—he'd been beat up pretty badly.

He required over 40 stitches to sew his side back together where the creature had injured him, but the vet said he would recover.

That little dog was a hero, and he was given the hero treatment, steaks for dinner, lots of love. He had turned from a complete coward to a hero when he saw Ellie was in danger. He had saved her.

I later ended up taking Ellie to a child psychologist to help her get over all this. I felt like I needed a shrink myself.

But the story doesn't end there. Ed and Gary finally went back to the house to get our car and stuff. They said they saw no blood nor any indication that the creature had been terribly injured. Nothing had been touched inside or out, except Ellie's favorite stuffed puppy was missing.

After moving everything but the furniture, the guys decided to go ahead and try to finish the harvest, which they did with no incidents.

Finally, after we'd rented a place in town, they went back and got all the furniture. They made one final trip to button up the house, when they found something really strange.

The creature had been back. They found fresh tracks going up to the grass. And sitting on the front steps was Ellie's little stuffed puppy.

On their way down the drive, on their final trip, Gary said he could see something big and black lying on the roof. That really gave me the creeps, wondering how many times it had been up there watching us and no one had known.

[15] Rockhounding with Uncle Hairy

You meet some interesting people in the backcountry, and Dave was one of the best. He was a young geologist, just like Jay in the story about Snowball.

I came upon Dave doing some field mapping while on my way out to check out a new fishing spot. We got to talking and before we realized it, several hours had passed.

Of course, our talk included Bigfoot, one of my favorite topics, and Dave told me quite the story.

My name's Dave, and this is the story of my last time rockhounding with my dad.

My dad was a field geologist, so we always ended up living in remote places, as he did geologic mapping for the USGS. At this particular time, we were living in the tiny town of Baker, Nevada, which is right next to Great Basin National Park.

I was 17 and in high school, close to graduating, commuting by bus to the nearby town of Ely.

My dad was a very self-sufficient guy and very safety conscious, as he was usually out in the middle of nowhere by himself.

He loved his job and loved being outdoors, and even though he worked outside all the time, he still wanted to be out on the weekends, so my sister and I grew up doing a lot of rockhounding with him. Sometimes my mom would go, but usually not.

Anyway, the story kind of starts with my dad's accident. He was working right at the edge of Great Basin National Park, doing some mapping, and he had this really bad accident.

If you know the area, it's along Strawberry Creek, you turn there by the Highway Department's shed and go on up the mountain on that little dirt road that kind of follows along the creek.

It's really pretty country, winds on up into the mountains and enters the park. We'd go up in there and picnic sometimes, lots of wild roses and aspens on up higher and along the creek.

So my dad was out there, working, and he'd driven up into this open meadow and parked his truck. It was on a gentle hill.

Like I said, my dad was very safety conscious, and he always made sure his truck was in gear and the emergency brake was set, which he also did on this particular day. He then got out and went around the back of the truck to get stuff from the rear. He was parked next to a thicket of wild roses.

Next thing he knew, he was on the ground with a broken leg, the truck had run over him. He said it felt like something had just shoved that truck right onto him. He didn't even have time to really react and get out of the way.

He felt the truck moving and tried to jump out of the way, but the truck knocked him down and ran over him, catching his leg under the tire, as he'd managed to get partway away from it.

The truck then rolled down the hill about 30 feet where it was stopped by a big boulder, denting the rear end.

My dad just lay there, stunned, and then he gradually realized he was seriously injured. This was back before people carried cell phones, so he was on his own. He could feel himself going into shock, and he knew he had to act quickly.

My dad was made of tough stuff, and he managed to actually crawl to the truck and hoist himself up into it with one leg.

He'd had the presence of mind to pick up a big stick, and he used that to push in the clutch and get the thing into first gear.

He slowly made his way back to the highway shed, where fortunately there were a couple of guys working. They took him to the hospital in Ely, and eventually he was transferred to the bigger hospital in Las Vegas.

He had a compound fracture and spent three months there, his leg was really messed up.

Fast forward to the day my mom goes to pick him up. His leg is healing well, and he's been in physical therapy and is dying to go home, he had a bad case of cabin fever, couldn't wait to get out.

He could now walk, but he had to take it easy. It would be some time before he was back to work. In the meantime, his company had fixed up his truck again, good as new.

So, now dad's home, and he's slowly recovering, walking around town and getting better. He'd been told to walk some, it would be good for him, so he did. He wanted to be outside anyway.

Mom had a job working with the Park Service, so she wasn't home a lot, and Dad was bored stiff.

So, Dad asked me if I wanted to go rockhounding with him. It was a Saturday and Mom was at work and I knew he'd go out alone if I said no, and nobody wanted that, so I said yes.

Off we went, back up to where he'd been injured along Strawberry Creek. He said he'd found some interesting rocks up there and wanted to go check it out, but I think he really wanted some closure on the whole thing, as close to being killed as he'd been.

I drove, and he told me where to go, and we went right back to the same spot he'd been hurt. We'd packed lunches and had snacks and water in our day packs, which was our standard operating procedure for rockhounding.

We soon went our separate ways. Nobody rock hounds together, you get off onto your own tangents, so there may be an hour or two before you reconnect, nothing to worry about.

But I was keeping an eye out for him, believe me. We'd keep track of each other by yelling. I'd yell, "Dad, hoo hoo hoo," and he'd answer, "hoo hoo hoo," kind of like owls but sometimes really loud if we weren't close together. Or he'd yell. "Dave, hoo hoo hoo," and I'd answer. You get the picture.

We got out there by late morning, so it was about mid-afternoon when we reconnected and had lunch at the truck. We should've tucked it in and gone home then.

Dad was walking pretty well, though, and it was just so nice to be out there he didn't want to go home yet. I felt like we should leave. He should be taking it easier his first time out.

We argued a bit, but he won, being the dad. I will always regret not insisting we go home then.

It was also then that we both smelled a really rancid odor. It was faint, but really rancid, like something dead.

Dad remarked that something had died and the wind had changed direction, that was why we could smell it now and not before. It made you want to throw up, even though it wasn't that strong.

Dad wanted to go back over the crest of a nearby hill and see what this boulder field he'd spotted was all about. Always the geologist.

So off he went, promising to be back within an hour or less. I will also always regret not going with him, but I was tired. I'd been out partying a bit the night before.

So, I waited at the truck, drinking coffee from our thermos and having some candy bars and just fiddling around.

Before long, I realized time was getting away from us, and he'd been gone over an hour. It was now getting towards late afternoon, and the sun would be setting, as it was late October and the days were getting shorter.

I decided to go looking for him and get us back home. Mom would be furious if we came in very late, as she hadn't wanted him out here in the first place.

I grabbed my coat and headed out towards that boulder field. I got to the crest of the hill and started yelling out, "Dad, hoo hoo hoo," hoping for an answer, but heard nothing.

I could see for quite a ways up on that ridge, and I stood there for a long time, trying to spot him. Nothing.

I decided that maybe he'd circled around to the truck, so I backtracked and went up onto another ridge where I could look down the other way. Still nothing. All this time I was calling out, "Dad, hoo hoo hoo," hoping for a response.

Now I was getting seriously worried. I went back to the truck, hoping he had come back while I was gone, but he hadn't. Now the sun was getting really low, and I estimated we had about fifteen minutes until sunset. You know, you can hold your hand up to the sun and estimate how many minutes until it sets by the number of fingers between it and the horizon, five fingers is about an hour.

I could picture my dad sitting somewhere on a rock, his leg messed up again, unable to walk, waiting for me to find him. And Mom was Irish and had a wonderful temper.

I had been yelling, "Dad, hoo hoo hoo," this entire time, over and over, then listening for a response. I yelled again, getting hoarse, standing there by the truck, and I'll be darned if I didn't hear something way off in the distance, and it sounded like it could maybe be, "Dave, hoo hoo hoo."

I grabbed my flashlight and headed for the boulder field again, the direction the sound had come from. When I got to the ridge, the sun had set, and I couldn't see very far for all the shadows.

I yelled again and was answered! It was Dad! I went running down the ridge towards the boulder field. I had to find him before it got really dark.

It was about a half-mile from the ridge to the big meadow filled with boulders, most of which looked to be about waist high.

I stopped a few times to yell and make sure I was heading in the right direction, and Dad would answer, "Dave, hoo hoo hoo."

But as I got closer, I kind of slowed down a bit. The voice just didn't sound quite right. It was kind of hollow, and I realized it was way louder than Dad could probably yell.

I wondered if he wasn't injured again and was stressed and it was affecting his voice. But I started to get a bit spooked, especially since it was now getting dark.

I stopped running and listened more carefully when the voice would answer me. I was now walking fast and nearly to the edge of the boulder field.

The voice was much much closer, but I soon figured out that it was staying a bit ahead of me. This really spooked me, 'cause if it were Dad, it would be stationary. He wouldn't be calling me and then walking away.

I now entered the area filled with boulders. It was slow going, as I had to work my way through and around them. I got about 30 feet in there and stopped and hooted for Dad.

"Dad, hoo hoo hoo."

I was answered, "Dave, hoo hoo hoo."

I yelled, "Dad, is that you? Are you OK?"

The answer came, "Dave, hoo hoo hoo."

I knew he could hear me, and for him to answer like that was creepy.

Something was wrong. Very wrong. He would normally say something like, "Over here."

I started backing up and got out of the boulders. I would go back and get Dad's rifle from the truck and come back. I'd heard Dad talk about a few escapades his colleagues had with n'er do wells out in the backcountry.

I was now deeply suspicious. Someone had harmed Dad and was now trying to bushwhack me.

I practically ran back up that ridge to the truck, looking over my shoulder the entire way. Dad always insisted that everyone had an extra set of keys, and now I was glad for this. I drove the truck on up to the ridge and parked it.

I grabbed Dad's rifle from its rack and loaded it, putting the little canvas pouch with extra shells into my pocket.

I then grabbed my flashlight and turned on the pickup lights so they'd shine down into the boulders, and headed back down.

I can honestly say it was the bravest thing I've ever done. My hands were literally shaking from fear and anger that someone had hurt my dad.

I ran back down the hill and entered the boulder field, rifle ready.

"Dad, hoo hoo hoo."

"Dave, hoo hoo hoo."

I very cautiously followed the voice for a bit. I wanted to sneak up on the guy, so I quit calling and turned off my flashlight.

I stood there for a bit and let my eyes adjust, as the moon was rising in the east, giving a bit of light. Then I started following the voice, for whoever it was hadn't given up.

And now I could smell that terrible rancid smell again, only now it was so strong it made me literally gag.

It kept calling, though now softly, "Dave, hoo hoo hoo. Dave, hoo hoo hoo."

I very slowly and cautiously followed the voice. I would get whoever had hurt my dad, make him tell me where Dad was, and maybe even shoot him. I was scared and frantic.

"Dave, hoo hoo hoo. Dave, hoo hoo hoo."

Now I was almost upon whoever was making the sound, and I was scared stiff, I mean the most scared I've ever been in my life, before or since.

The voice stopped. All was quiet.

I knew the ambush was ready and I lifted my rifle to shoot, hoping they wouldn't sneak around from behind. I just stood there for the longest time, and then I heard the voice, only now it was ahead of me a bit again.

I stepped forward towards it and nearly fell over my dad. He was lying there, and I knelt down by him, and asked, "Dad, are you OK?"

When I touched him I knew instantly he was dead, he was cold. I just kneeled there by him for the longest time. The voice had stopped and I was in a state of shock.

Then I came back around and knew I had to get him and myself out of there. I was a big kid, six foot two, and strong, and I was able to hoist him over my shoulder, as he wasn't a really big guy.

As I was turning around with him on my shoulder, that's when I saw the eyes. There were two sets, they glowed a deep red with a glow that wasn't from the moonlight, it was somehow coming from inside the eyes. And these eyes were a good seven feet off the ground.

They were maybe 20 feet away, and the boulders blocked me from seeing their bodies, but I could make out shadows of heads that were huge and seemed to have a ridge on the top. They were swaying, like they were trying to see me better without me seeing them.

I think I then just totally detached, seeing my dad and now these huge things. I don't know how I did it, but I struggled through the boulders and on up that hill with him on my shoulder, the rifle in my other hand, half-running, and ready to fight.

I followed the lights of the pickup, and when I got back, I gently placed him into the truck bed and covered him with my jacket.

I then got the hell out of there as fast as I could, driving like a maniac down the dirt road that follows Strawberry Creek.

I got back to the highway and headed into Ely. I didn't want my mom to see him like this. I drove to a gas station there and asked them to call the cops, which they did.

As soon as the police showed up, I basically collapsed. I could barely talk. We ended up at the hospital, where they took my dad's body and put me into the ER and called my mom, who came and got me.

The next day, I did a full police report and the hospital did an autopsy. My dad had died from a heart attack. They estimated the time to be late afternoon. I told no one about the voice and what I'd seen. I never told my mom or sis.

I won't go into the effect all this had on me and my mom and sister, but it was a difficult time, to be sure. We eventually left Baker and moved to Delta, Utah, which is about 100 miles to the east, where my mom got a job with the school district.

My sister went on to college and I joined the army, and then later went to college. My mom eventually remarried.

Every so often I think of that day and wonder what exactly happened. Did my dad have a heart attack because he saw these creatures and it scared him literally to death?

Or did they come upon his body and very compassionately lure me down there so I would find him, mimicking his voice?

Were they the ones who pushed his truck in the first place, causing him to break his leg? I somehow feel they weren't out to get me, 'cause after seeing them, I wouldn't have stood a chance. That rifle would have felt like nothing to them, they were so big.

I guess I'll never know.

And that's the story of my last rockhounding trip with my dad.

[16] Bad Vibes in the Badlands

* *

Even though I'm a guide in Colorado, I sometimes like to go check out new places. I was over on Boulder Mountain in Utah, doing some lake fishing when I met Jack, another guide.

Jack and I instantly hit it off. We were kindred souls with the same obsession. He invited me home to his little cabin for dinner, where I met his lovely wife, Susan, who told me the following story.

I always go to the same places to take my dogs out, every day. Mostly because I let them off leash and I like to know what's up, I like to have everything scoped out and no worries about them running.

Now that we're here in Boulder, I go out on that road that heads up Long Canyon, but this story happened near where we then lived, in Dubois, Wyoming.

I used to always go to this place where you drive up onto a hill and you can see out, which I liked. You can stand there at the end of this little spur that takes off another dirt road, and just see out forever.

It's the badlands region just out of town, you may know it. It's very pretty in sort of a desolate remote way. Kind of like here, come to think of it.

Anyway, I took my three dogs out there nearly every day. There were a couple of other spots I'd go to, but this was my favorite. It kind of inspired me, I like wild places.

I'm kind of a habitual person, I guess. I would always go the same time of day, early afternoon (I'm a retired nurse), and I'd always park my pickup at the same place. Then we'd walk down and around the hills, kind of always the same way.

The dogs got used to it and that was nice, because if one of them took off for a bit I didn't worry, they knew exactly where to find me. But they're really good dogs and would take off only if they saw a rabbit, then they'd come right back. We even eventually wore a little trail into the hills. Not much vegetation, just dirt.

Well, one day, the dogs were a bit ahead of me, running down this hill, and I couldn't see around to where they were, but they were on our little trail. They'd do this, run ahead a bit sometimes. They loved running out there.

But I have one who sticks by my side, her name's Daisy, and all of a sudden she stopped and started growling. She couldn't see the other two, Sweet Pea and Rowdy, nor could I.

Daisy stopped and growled and I listened to her. These dogs are smart. She once warned me of a mountain lion, so I always listen.

Seconds later, the other two came running back to me as fast as they could, scared to death, tails between their legs and their ears back. I listen to them, too, so we all turned around and went back to the truck.

They abandoned me for that truck, running back as fast as they could, except Daisy, and I could tell she wanted to run, too. They were truly scared.

It made me feel really creepy, and I kept looking over my shoulder. My bet was some guy out shooting or something. I would rarely see anyone out there, but you never know. But I'd never seen them run like this, and I couldn't hear anyone shooting.

So we went home and they were very subdued. The next day, we went back out there and they wouldn't even get out of the truck.

I sat there for a bit, looking around, but I couldn't for the life of me see or hear anything. We drove out to the other side of town and they were just fine, and we had a nice walk.

I mentioned it to my husband that evening and he didn't like it. He said I should stay away from the badlands, something was out there.

He was still working as a fishing guide, and he worried about me hiking around alone, though I told him I wasn't alone, I had three dogs. But he still worried. Dubois is right on the edge of the Wind River Range, and those mountains are full of grizzly bears.

So I agreed to not go back to the badlands for awhile, maybe a grizzly was out there. It was pretty unlikely, as there wasn't any cover for them nor food.

So we stayed away for a week or so, but then I missed it. Every other place was more restricted, I'd end up at some rancher's fence or the river. I wanted to go back out to my favorite place.

So, we finally went back out. The dogs seemed hesitant at first, but they were OK, and we had a nice walk. I figured it was some kind of wildlife that had scared them, but I'd never seen them act like that, although they had never been around bears.

I told my husband we were going back out there, and he didn't like it, but there wasn't much he could do.

We started going back out there every day, and I gradually forgot about the whole incident.

But then, one day I'll never forget, we'd been down around the bottom of the hills, when the dogs started acting strange again. They wanted to go back to the truck.

So we started back, and all of a sudden I got this really strange feeling that something was watching me. I can't describe it. It was just as creepy as it can get.

It made me want to run, but I forced myself not to, as that can trigger an attack reaction in some wild animals, like mountain lions.

The dogs ran back, except Daisy, and she started growling again. I walked as fast as I could.

We weren't all that close to the truck when this started, and it took awhile to get to the top of the hill. The badlands are just a bunch of steep eroded hills, up and down.

I was almost to the top of the hill, and I could see Sweet Pea and Rowdy at the truck, when Daisy started whining and took off.

That was so unlike her, she would give her life for me—so I thought, anyway. I stopped and turned around, and what I saw just boggled my mind.

There, way down at the bottom of the hill, was this black creature, and it was just standing there watching us. But as I watched it, it started running right up the hill towards me.

It was incredibly fast, it ran on two legs, and it looked like a giant gorilla. It had gotten a good third of the way up the hill before my instincts kicked in and I started running.

The only thing I can think of to compare it to is a cloud shadow moving before the sun, it just floated across the ground, so fast.

I was terrified. I opened the truck door in a flash and whoosh, the dogs were inside and me behind them. I managed to start it and take off just as this thing approached. It actually slapped the back of the truck as I took off, it was that close.

Now here's the bad part. I usually will park so I can just drive away. I never like to have to turn around on my way out. I guess it's just a safety habit I've gotten into over the years.

But this one time, I had parked facing up the road, and not down. I have no idea why, it was not at all like me.

You have to picture this little spur road coming off another back road, and I'd parked where I was facing out to the back road, but I would have to back up a bit to turn and get on it to go downhill. Bad bad mistake.

I was so scared I didn't want to have to stop and back up with this thing right behind me, so I just gunned it up the hill. I'd never even been up this road before, but it looked like it led on up the crest of the badlands and into the hills above. Maybe mountains above would be a better statement.

I found out immediately it was rough and rutted as I bounced along as fast as I could. I couldn't see the thing in my rearview mirror, but as fast as it could run, I wasn't taking any chances. I guess I was just running on raw reaction. I figured I needed to get away, and I could deal with where later.

The dogs were in the cab with me. It's an extended cab, and they were all huddled in the back seat like a bunch of scared rabbits. I've never seen them like this before or since.

I bounced my little Toyota Tacoma on up that hill, just beating the heck out of it for a good couple of miles or more before I stopped. I'd come to a little clearing. I was now up in the thick scrub.

It was a good place to turn around, so I thought. I pulled off the road and got turned around, and then I was instantly stuck.

It had apparently rained up there enough to make it muddy. It was gumbo, but you couldn't see how muddy it was for the leaves and all. The road itself had dried out.

I have four-wheel drive, and I put it into 4x4, but the more I tried, the stucker I got. I was buried in mud clear down to my hubs. Now I was really really scared because I was helpless if that thing was still following me.

I knew I had to act fast before it caught up with me, so I jumped out and started grabbing up sticks lying around, putting them under the tires for traction.

This didn't help a bit. I got back out and looked around for anything I could use, but there weren't even any rocks small enough to drag under the wheels, just large boulders.

It was then that I heard the howl from hell. That thing was still coming up the road and it wasn't all that far away!

My heart was beating so fast I thought I was having a heart attack. Like I said, I'm a retired nurse, so I know what that's like, I've seen it. Oh God almighty, I was scared.

I jumped back into the truck, then I noticed them— my floor mats! I quickly grabbed both from the cab and jumped out, sticking them under the rear tires.

I then slowly drove forward, but it wasn't much before I was stuck again, but not as deep. And I'd made a little progress!

I jumped out again and pulled the mats from the mud and put them up under the tires again. I did this several times until I could finally gun it and was free, back on the road again! What a feeling that was!

I just left the mats there, in the mud. But now I had to figure out how to deal with this huge creature. I knew it could probably pick up my truck if it wanted, it looked that strong, and I was certain to meet it coming up the road. My mind went blank, what could I do? I had no weapons or any way to protect myself.

I drove really slow, because I needed time to figure out a plan of action. I thought about trying to hide in the bushes, of just driving off the road back into the scrub somehow, but I knew I'd get stuck again. Besides, the scrub was so thick I don't think I could get in it to hide. And there was no way I would abandon the truck to try to hide, that would be suicidal.

So there we were, me and the dogs, slowly driving back down the road, wondering what was next, terrified and alone.

You can only imagine how I felt when I came around a corner and saw a small tree blocking the road! It obviously wasn't there when we went up, or we wouldn't have gone up!

This was the scrub oak zone, and there weren't many trees, but here was a small aspen, blocking my way. It had been dragged onto the road.

That's when the adrenalin rush took over and I knew it was a survival situation. This creature intended to harm us.

My pickup has pretty good clearance, and I just hit the accelerator. I would've peeled rubber if it hadn't been a dirt road. I gunned it and we just crashed right through and over that tree, limbs and all.

I could hear it cracking against the bottom of my truck, and I was worried I'd done some damage, but I kept on going.

It was then that something big crashed into the back of my pickup. I looked in the rearview mirror and I could see another aspen tree half riding in the bed, but a lot bigger one.

I found out later it had dented the tailgate and side of the bed, so it had to have been thrown really hard to do that. And just then another hit, but this one came right through my back window like a spear, shattering the glass.

If I hadn't had an extended cab, it would've come crashing right onto my head, but it stopped a few inches behind me.

I was now going as fast as I dared, the dogs were on the floor, and the one tree had bounced out, but the spear-tree was still with me, and there was glass everywhere. I really thought a couple of times I would lose control. I didn't dare stop.

I finally got back down to the badlands with no more incidents, and I was so relieved, but I didn't slow down a bit. I was soon back in the little town of Dubois, and I drove home.

My husband wouldn't be home yet, but I really needed him. So I called his work on my cell phone, and they sent him home. He fortunately had just come in from fishing with some clients.

I pulled into the drive and quickly got the dogs into the house. They were scared to death. I then assessed the situation. My truck was a mess. I didn't even know where to start.

And how would you explain to your insurance company that your truck had been vandalized by what looked to be a Bigfoot?

My husband came home not long after. I had locked myself in the house, even though we lived right in town. My pickup was a disaster, and so was I.

But now I was scared it would find me, had somehow followed me and knew where I lived. I think I was suffering from PTSD. The dogs hid under the bed, but they finally came out when Jack (my husband) came home.

He was incredulous, but he seemed to believe me. He went out and cleaned up the glass and everything on my truck.

He said the tree that had come through my window had marks on it where it was broken off at the base. It seemed to have been twisted off, which was hard to believe, as it was a good eight inches thick. I think that's what tipped the scales and made him a believer.

The next day was Saturday, and Jack got up early, which was unlike him, as he usually slept in a bit. I hadn't slept all night. He said he was going up there to see if he could spot the Bigfoot or whatever it was.

I begged him not to, but he had already rounded up three of his buddies. They all had pickups and rifles. I was scared stiff. A good friend came over and spent the day with me.

Off they went. I worried about them all day, but when they came back that evening they hadn't seen a thing. They'd been all over the badlands and even on up into the timber. And yes, one of them had even gotten stuck.

But they had found something of interest, and Jack showed me the digital photos. It was a tree that had been ripped from the ground, roots and all, not far from where I'd been stuck. Whatever did it was very strong. And Jack had found my floor mats and retrieved them.

Word soon got out around town, and a number of people came by to look at my truck. Come to find out, Bigfoot had been historically sighted in the Wind Rivers, there were a number of stories, so I wasn't as foolish looking as I thought I would be.

And the Shoshone Indians had a number of oral histories about the creature.

That was all it took for Jack. He worked outdoors and was afraid he might run into it, too. He made some calls to friends and got a job as a fishing guide in, of all places, southeast Utah, fishing the lakes on Boulder Mountain. We were gone within two weeks, since we were renting. I didn't argue one bit, as I was glad to go.

My friend called me later and told me the creature had been sighted not long after down along the river. The whole town was stirred up, but that was the last time anyone saw it, so I guess it went away.

[17] Fire on the River

· ·

This story was told by a guy named Marty over a campfire in the great fishing country of the Gunnison River in Colorado, although it actually happened a number of miles away on the Colorado River.

Marty was from the nearby town of Hotchkiss, where he owns an apple orchard. His girlfriend in the story is now his wife, and she and Marty run the orchard.

I find this story somewhat disturbing. Does Bigfoot know how to start and use fire? If so, there could be many implications, especially if the Big Guy were to get angry. Were the Bigfoot on the river territorial and trying to get rid of everyone? I try not to dwell on it.

My girlfriend Kelly and I were both working in Grand Junction, Colorado, and we decided we'd do a river trip down the Colorado, which flows right through the middle of town.

We both worked for the Colorado State Extension Service there. I worked in the horticulture department and she worked as a 4-H support person, helping the 4-H agents.

Anyway, there's a boat ramp near the little town of Loma, on the outskirts of Junction, and it's a popular place to put in and raft or canoe on down through Ruby and Horsethief canyons, getting out just before the major rapids in Westwater Canyon. That ramp is where we put in for our trip.

It's typically a two-day journey, but we decided to do it in three, spending a day hiking around and exploring the country. We had a small raft and plenty of food and beer and whatever you might need for a three-day trip. So off we went. We were really looking forward to it.

It's a quiet stretch of water, with the only real rapids being at a place called Black Rocks, where the river cuts into Precambrian basement rock that's several billion years old, and one can easily portage around if they want. Most of the river is calm enough that even canoeists run it.

It doesn't take long until you're in Horsethief Canyon, a beautiful deep redrock canyon. It's paradise. I remember seeing a big hawk flying over the river with a live snake in its talons. I've never seen anything like that before or since.

We floated on down the river and found a nice beach to spend our first night on. The sky was clear, and it was just surreal, the stars were so thick.

We were camped on a little estuary that had cut into the bank, making a small island with lots of willows. We had a quiet and restful night, happy to be outdoors.

The next day, we decided to float on down a few miles and then find a camp spot and spend the rest of the day hiking. The canyon had opened up and we knew there were several large canyons we could access on foot. One was called Mee Canyon, I can't recall the others. Mee Canyon had a giant alcove in it I wanted to go see.

We hadn't seen many people on the river so far. It was late fall, and a lot of people were back at work, having used up their vacation time.

So, we pulled over after a short time and beached our raft and made a lunch and took off. We were on the outside of a long sweeping turn in the river, and the inside was a bit faster than the outside.

As we took off, we climbed up a small bench just as a canoe came down the river. It was carrying a boy, probably around 12, in the bow, and what we took to be his dad, an older man, in the back. They got into that faster water and immediately flipped their canoe.

We watched, but there was nothing we could do. They were hanging onto the canoe and managed to flip it back over and get back into it. We were happy they made it, and they went on down the river.

We did notice a large party of seven or so canoes come down behind them shortly after, and that made us feel a bit better. We knew the inexperienced pair would have help if they needed it. We thought no more about it, and went on our hike, having a wonderful day, even though we didn't make it to Mee Canyon.

But when we got back to our camp, we discovered the man and his son had stopped just below us and set up their tent. This wasn't something we wanted, as we were there for privacy and to get away from people.

Their tent was only maybe 100 feet from where we had left the raft. It looked like they'd had to backtrack to get that close to us. They must have pulled their canoe back up the river or something.

It was almost dark, and we debated whether or not to float on down the river a bit. We decided it was too late, so we set up camp and just hoped they'd be quiet. We were both pretty disgusted, as camping etiquette says to not bunch together, especially when there's tons of places to camp.

We had dinner, and it wasn't long till the coyotes started in. I love hearing them, they have such a wide range of vocals, and you can tell they love to sing. In fact, the old-timers called them "song dogs."

It sounded like a large pack, but I know from experience two or three can sound that way. I've watched them sing many times through binoculars. I've actually even had them come into my camp and yowl and yip in the middle of the night, right by my tent.

But all of a sudden, they stopped and it went dead quiet. I was surprised, because they seemed to be really having a great time, and they just stopped, all together, like that. It was strange.

I perked up. Maybe there was a mountain lion in the area. That would be something we might want to be aware of. I talked to Kelly about it, and she agreed we should be extra cautious, not leave camp. We agreed to stick together.

We sat there in the dark for a bit. We hadn't lit our lantern or made a fire, as we were star-gazing. Kelly remarked that it was weird that even the frogs and crickets were quiet.

I hadn't noticed, but now that she pointed it out, it did seem weird. We both huddled together a bit closer, which I certainly didn't mind.

But all of a sudden we could hear our neighbors, and it sounded like they were arguing. They had actually been pretty quiet until then, and we'd kind of forgot they were there. We could see smoke. They had built a fire.

We could hear the boy yelling, and he sounded scared more than angry. Then his dad was talking loud, but we couldn't make out what they were saying. Then all was quiet. The smoke disappeared, like they'd put out the fire.

Soon, the crickets and frogs began making their night sounds, and the coyotes started howling again, though now further in the distance.

We went to bed and had a peaceful night. We were really tired from our day hike, so I think things could've picked up and we wouldn't have heard a thing.

I'm an amateur photographer, so I always get up really early when I'm out like that, so I can shoot the sunrise. Photographers call sunrise and sunset the magic hours.

Kelly was still sleeping, and I was up, just sitting on a nearby rock in the early dawn, drinking coffee, when I heard our neighbors talking. I was really surprised to hear them up so early.

I then realized the voices were getting fainter. They must already be on the river! This really surprised me, nobody gets on the river when it's still nearly dark.

I went ahead and filmed a beautiful sunrise. Cirrus clouds. We were in for a weather change in the next day or two, I thought.

The clouds were really nice, turning different shades of pink and orange as the sun rose, casting reflections in the river. I was in photographer's heaven.

Soon, Kelly was up, and we made some pancakes over our little camp stove and had more coffee. This was the life. We were loving it. This would be our last day, and we hated to go home and back to work.

We soon had camp packed up and were on our way. It was still early, as we wanted to get an early start so we could maybe get in another hike. It wasn't that far out to Westwater. My sister would pick us up in my pickup.

As we floated down the river, Kelly, who has a very sensitive nose, remarked that she could smell smoke. It took awhile, but I could soon smell it, too. It seemed to be coming from down the river, the direction we were floating. It was too strong and acrid to be a campfire. I wondered if the rancher at Westwater wasn't maybe burning his ditches.

As we floated further downriver, the smoke got thicker. We both got more concerned. A river-bottom fire would be hard to deal with, as there was no place to go.

Even though the canyons had opened up quite a bit, we still had cliffs to our right. The open bottom areas to our left on the other side of the river were thick with willows and tamarisk and big cottonwood trees.

We decided to pull over and see if the smoke got worse, rather than drifting right smack into trouble.

I beached the raft on the right side of the river, thinking it would be safer, as the fire would surely come up the left, where all the vegetation was.

We sat there awhile, waiting. Before long, a canoe had joined us, carrying a married couple. We all sat and talked, wondering what was going on.

Our talk soon stopped. The winds were picking up! What had been an early morning breeze now was turning into a good 10 to 15 m.p.h. wind. A storm was definitely coming in.

The smoke was getting thicker. We had no place to go, so we just sat there and watched. Soon we could see flames coming up around the bend, a quarter mile away.

Sure enough, the fire was on the left side of the river. At least we were on the safer side to be on.

The fire was being whipped by the winds, and we could now hear its roar. It was something to behold, coming right at us.

Then Kelly let out a yell and pointed. Running ahead of the fire, just barely out of its reach, were two large men, or large somethings, and they looked like they were wearing football uniforms.

They were totally black, from head to toe. It was hard to make out any features or detail, as they were enveloped by smoke. The fire was nearly upon them!

At that point, I could hardly breathe, and it felt like my hair was going to catch on fire. Kelly yelled, "Get in the water!"

We all jumped in, nothing but our heads sticking out. Of course, at that point, no one could see the figures and what had become of them. I wondered if they hadn't also jumped in the river.

The fire was soon past us, the winds whipping it rapidly along. I was again able to breathe, though the acrid smell of still-smoking vegetation made my eyes water and my lungs ache. But we were still alive.

There's no better way to bond with people than to go through something like that together. Kelly and I are still friends with the couple that had the canoe. We still speculate on who the black figures were and what became of them.

I was glad the canoeists were there, because frankly, I was worried our raft had melted enough to be unsafe or to even flat-out sink. But it seemed fine. The couple stayed with us the rest of the way out to make sure we were OK.

So, we all floated on down the river together, wrapping wet t-shirts around our faces to cut down the smoke we inhaled on the way, as the vegetation was still smoking and there were little fires everywhere. The wind made the going hard, and I had to row.

We were soon at a big sand bar, where we stopped. We didn't like what we saw, and we had to see if anyone needed help. It looked like an entire camp had burned.

The whole place smoldered, and we got out and walked around, trying not to burn our soles, stepping on only the sandy places.

There, on the bar, were about a dozen tents, all of various colors—red, blue, green, even orange—and each was melted into the ground from the fire. Some were still melting, as nylon doesn't burn very well.

It was an eerie sight, and I know the others were thinking the same thing I was—what if we find a body, or more than one?

As we walked around the camp site, it was obvious that whoever was there had left in a hurry. All kinds of things were scattered around.

I found a woman's makeup purse, and inside were a lipstick and a hairbrush, both melted into the purse itself. There were sandals melted into the ground, and even melted camp chairs, only the metal left.

After we had thoroughly walked around and made sure there was no one there, we were soon back on the river, quiet and subdued. It wasn't long until we reached the takeout and ranger station at Westwater.

We weren't prepared for what awaited us. There was a small group of people, maybe 20, and two rangers, with a state trooper arriving the same time we did.

One of the rangers came over to us as we were all pulling our boats from the water and told us not to leave. She wanted statements from us. They were trying to figure out what had happened. We assumed the fire was still burning its way up the river.

My sister was waiting in my pickup, so we loaded the boat and our gear, then sat on the tailgate, talking. After awhile, the rangers took our names and phone numbers, saying they would call us in a day or two.

They were overwhelmed, trying to make arrangements for the large canoeing party whose camp had burned. I noticed the man and his son standing a bit aside from the group. They looked very serious and didn't talk to each other.

So, we went on home. Our idyllic trip had turned into a bit of a nightmare. We were lucky to be alive. Kelly and I both had lung problems for several days, they would periodically ache. We finally recovered.

It was a week later when we got a call from a law-enforcement ranger, asking if he could come and interview us. Two rangers showed up the next evening at our house, asking questions. We didn't really have many answers, but we told them what we knew. They were especially interested in the story about the man and his son arguing.

We asked for more information about the fire, but they couldn't say anything, since it was still under investigation, but they did say it was now out. They soon got up to leave, as we really didn't have much to tell them.

But that's when Kelly stopped them and told them we'd forgotten something. She proceeded to tell them about the dark figures running ahead of the fire.

The rangers told us they'd heard the same story from the canoeist couple and had no idea what it could be. They were just as puzzled as we were.

Several months later, Kelly got a call from Rich and Jeanie, the canoeists we'd met. They wanted to have dinner with us. They had some news about the fire.

Rich worked for the Tammy Coalition, a group trying to eradicate the invasive tamarisk from the river, and he knew everyone in the local boating world.

Word had finally come down about the fire, as one of their members was a friend of one of the rangers, and you know how that goes.

Rich told us the following story. The man and his son who had capsized their canoe had seen a strange creature along the bank shortly before they capsized.

That's why they were on the inside of the current, they were trying to stay as far away from this thing as possible, as it seemed to be paralleling them on the river, and it was fast. It must have gone below where we were standing on the upper bench, as we didn't see anything.

The creature had gone on down the river, and they were scared, thinking it was looking for them. They had seen us and decided to backtrack and camp close to us for safety. They hadn't wanted to alarm us, so they kept to themselves.

But that evening, about the same time we'd heard everything go quiet, there had been a small fire set next to their tent. The dad had discovered it and was able to immediately put it out.

He thought his son had been trying to light a fire, which he had ordered him not to do. He didn't want to draw any kind of attention to themselves. The son swore he hadn't done it. That next morning, they had awakened to strange noises, so they got up and left.

I found it strange that we had heard nothing, but maybe the creature hadn't seen us. Anyway, the pair went on down the river, and this creature was soon once again paralleling them. But now there were two of the creatures.

By now, the man and boy were scared to death. They were a bit ahead of the creatures, though, and they soon came upon the camp with the large canoe party. These were the people who had gone down the river right after them the previous day, but the dad and son hadn't seen them, as they'd pulled into the willows to hide from the creature following them.

The pair decided to stop and seek safety in numbers, although everyone was still asleep because it was so early.

They beached their canoe and went into the camp. But all of a sudden the grass around the camp was on fire!

Fortunately, they were able to yell and get everyone up and into the canoes and down the river before it turned into a disaster.

At this point, some of the party was suspecting the man and boy had set the fire. The timing seemed just too coincidental—they show up just as a fire starts. But what would be their motive? No one could figure it out.

Everyone was soon at Westwater, and by now the rangers could see smoke rising from up river. We showed up not too long later.

So, things weren't looking good for the man and his son. They decided to go ahead and tell everyone about the creatures tailing them, but it just sounded too fantastic for the rangers, and no one else had seen anything.

They arrested the dad, and the boy was taken into custody and then released to his mom.

The dad was charged and released on bond. Now law enforcement took over the investigation, and that's when we were interviewed.

Come to find out, based on our testimony, the man was released and the charges dropped. They now had four people testifying that they had seen two strange "men" running from the fire. He was now being looked upon as a hero, having awakened everyone in time to get away from the fire.

I don't know what came of their investigation, but I doubt if it went any further. We were glad that whatever it was had left us alone, even though we didn't understand why.

So that's the story. I bet the man and his son never go down the river again, and I doubt if we will. And I bet this one went into the truth is stranger than fiction ranger files.

[18] The Bigfoot Runes

· ·

This is the only story in this collection that didn't come to me over the smoke of a campfire or from a friend.

I was contacted by the professor in this story when he somehow heard that I was working on this book. He wanted my opinion on the matter.

I found his story fascinating and asked his permission to publish it, which he gave, although he says he's thinking about writing a full-on book on the topic, depending on how things shake out.

(Once again, all names and locations have been changed, in case you feel an urge to go find this cave.)

My story has not yet ended, but let me tell you what's happened so far. My name is Bryce and I'm a professor at a large university in the western U. S. I have a PhD in Linguistics from Princeton University.

Some think that linguistics is when you can speak a lot of languages, but it's really the study of languages. It's actually a very interesting and somewhat difficult field.

Here's how the story begins. I was in my office, grading papers, when I got a call from the department secretary. She said I had a visitor downstairs, should she send him up?

This was a really unusual call for her to make, since normally people just came up to my office door and knocked. She never screened our visitors. I knew something was up, and this was her way of telling me.

I thought for a moment, then asked, "Judy, can you talk?" She replied that she couldn't. So I told her to stall him for a few minutes while I came downstairs. That way if something were fishy, we could steer him away together.

My office is in one of the older buildings on campus. It's very picturesque, a three-story stone building with ivy growing up the sides, just like in the photos of ivy-league universities.

Before I knew it, I was hosting one of the least likely people to ever sit in an ivy-covered university building. Why I let him into my office I'm not sure, because he certainly didn't look like anyone I would ever have anything in common with, or even be likely to associate with, for that matter.

My guest was wearing green khaki clothing from head to toe, along with worn army-type boots. He was rough looking and scruffy with a short unkempt beard, and his longish dark hair was graying.

His face was tanned and leathery, like someone who had spent their lives outdoors. And he had a big knife strapped to his belt.

I asked him to sit down, and he looked distinctly un-comfortable. He sat on the edge of his chair, kind of leaning over my desk. I had no idea why he was here, he looked to be in his mid-forties, certainly not a typical student.

He introduced himself as Sam and got right to the point.

"Prof, you study languages, right?"

I assured him I did.

"Are you able to crack codes, you know, like maybe something that looks like it might be a written language?"

I told him that it might be possible, depending on the amount of information available.

He sat there for awhile, as if assessing whether or not he wanted to continue. I guess he decided he did, because he then asked, "Can you keep a secret?"

I assured him I could, but it would depend on what kind of secret, and I couldn't make any promises until I knew more.

This made him even more uncomfortable, and I thought he might get up and leave at that point. I was actually kind of hoping he would, to tell the truth. I wasn't interested in some Indiana Jones adventure, and this was starting to remind me of the start of a bad movie.

He now leaned back in his chair and said, "I'm kind of an anarchist kind of guy. I don't fit in, in case you didn't notice. I've had kind of a rough life, and I sure ain't no edu-cated man, like you. But, I know how to survive on my own. I do odd jobs to make it, and I hunt my own food. I know we come from different worlds, but I would really like your help. I've found something that's really interesting, and I'm totally out of my league."

I was beginning to wonder if this wasn't some kind of practical joke by some of my students. Maybe they were filming it. It wouldn't be the first time a prof had been pranked. I went along with it, kind of surreptitiously looking around my office for a camera, trying not to be obvious.

"I'll help if I can. Go ahead."

"Prof, promise me you'll keep quiet about this. It's just between you and me, OK?"

"OK, but you can call me Bryce instead of Prof."

"OK, Prof, that's a deal. Have a few minutes?"

I looked at my watch. My next class was in two hours. The papers I was grading could wait. I nodded that I did.

Sam then reached into one of the pockets of the fisherman's vest he was wearing, its pockets stuffed with who knows what, probably matches and survival gear.

He pulled out a little notebook and handed it to me. "Take a look, Prof, and tell me what you think."

I carefully opened the small notebook, which looked like it had been so well-used that the pages were nearly coming off the small spiral binder.

The first page had some kind of diary entry, something like—spg, falow gzly ck 3 mi e 2 jagd rck, lft..."—that kind of thing. Sam said to turn the page, so I did.

The next page had three simple connected lines drawn on it. They looked like some sort of rune.

I turned to the next page, same thing, but different. Also the next and the next. Runic-looking inscriptions, each different. I pointed out the obvious, that they looked like some sort of runes.

"Just what exactly is a rune?" Sam asked.

"Well," I explained, "In short, they're a sort of alphabet. They preceded the Latin alphabet we now use. There were a number of runic alphabets, but the better-known ones were used in Scandinavia, as well as in Germanic countries. They're a simple way of creating letters. I'm not a runic expert, but I do have some experience with them from graduate school, although it's been awhile."

Sam replied, "Well, let me tell you more. I was up hunting in the..." He paused, then added, "I can tell you more about where later, but let's just say it's a very rugged area with lots of limestone caves."

"Anyway, I tend to try and get into areas where nobody else goes, because that's where the game is. Deer are smart, they know where to hide. It was last October, and no, I wasn't poaching, I had a legit license."

The way he said this made me think he did a lot of poaching. He continued.

"I'm a bow hunter. Part of the challenge is hunting the old way. I'm a purist, and I hate modern hunters, they're just a bunch of posers. I won't go into that, but I bow hunt, which means I'm very quiet and stealthy.

"I was way way back in there, in country so wild I bet nobody's been in there since the Indians. That's just me, I like wild country.

"Anyway, I was walking along really quiet when I saw what you see on the second page there. It was carved into an aspen tree. I stopped to look at it. Since I was so remote, I was kind of surprised to see anything man-made.

"I thought maybe it was made by some sheepherder, you know, they have a tradition of carving in aspen trees. They get bored and carve all kinds of stuff. But it wasn't really old, you can tell by the growth of the tree. A tree will try to scar over the cut, but it was relatively fresh, and anyway, this wasn't sheepherding country.

"It was thick fir and spruce, with a few aspen and a rough understory. Not easy going. And bear country. No sheepherder in his right mind would run sheep there, you'd lose them all the first day, if not to the country, to the bears.

"So, I decided I'd write it down and see if I could figure it out later. I thought that maybe it was some kind of code or marker made by another hunter to find his way around. So I put it in my little book. I put everything in my little book.

"I was now following a little path. It was just a little winding path through the thick forest where the leaves and all had been beat down enough you could walk easier. An animal path.

"I hadn't gone more than 50 feet when I found that second mark, or rune, as you call it. I copied it into my book. I thought, this is getting interesting. But I sure as heck didn't want to run into anyone.

"And now, a third. All of these right along that animal path, carved into aspen trees. I kept walking along, and for some reason, I started getting the willies. I felt exposed, even though I was in a deep forest. Not too many aspens, as they need light, and the fir trees were getting too thick.

"I decided to step off the path and try to parallel it from in the brush. Hard to do, but it felt safer. I was beginning to wonder if I hadn't stumbled onto some kind of pot growers deal, and they are very dangerous."

Now Sam shifted in his seat and paused, as if he'd forgotten himself and was reassessing the situation to see if I could be trusted. I was already caught up in his story.

I asked him if he wanted some coffee, and he said yes, so I started a cup in my little espresso machine. I then told him to go on, his story was very interesting. He continued.

"Well, Prof, I was getting nervous, I can tell you. I followed alongside that little path and would find more trees with runes and copy them down, then get back off the path. It was easy to find them, 'cause like I said, there weren't that many aspens.

"This went on for a good mile, a long mile, winding in and out of trees and bushes and snags. I now had a good bunch of those runes in my little book, as you can see."

He paused while I handed him a cup of coffee. I was more and more intrigued by his story.

"Now, Prof, this is the part where you're likely to say I'm making this up, but I have something else I'd like to show you."

At this point, Sam pulled out a small pocket-sized digital camera, turned it on, and handed it to me.

"Be careful, Prof, these are the originals, and I don't have any way to make copies. I traded a nice Dutch oven for that camera. I figured it might come in handy someday, and it has. Push that little button on the left and you can scan through the photos."

I took the camera and carefully started scanning through what looked like photos taken indoors, vague and fuzzy, but I could make out an entire series of the runic figures.

Then, I could make out an entire wall of runes, then pages from a book. It reminded me of the Codex Runicus, a manuscript from around 1300 A.D. containing one of the oldest and best preserved texts written entirely in runes.

"Sam, this is amazing! It looks like you found a bunch of them on a wall in a cave and in a book or something?"

"Can you make anything out?" he asked.

"I don't know. They're too small on the camera to really tell. I need to download them on my computer before I can make any sense of them. They're too small."

"I need to know I can really trust you before you download anything, Prof."

I replied, "I understand that, but if I don't download them, I can't be of any help. What in the world could I possibly do with them?"

He didn't say a word, but nodded his head.

"Look," I said, why not take these to the local photo shop and have them put the photos on two discs, one for you and one for me. They deal with proprietary stuff all the time."

I continued, "Just have them print out a statement saying you own the copyright, and I have permission only to examine them, not to show them to anyone else or to use them in any other manner. I'll sign it when you bring the disc. Our secretary can witness it. That should work."

Sam relaxed and sipped his coffee for a bit, then said he would do that, and would I like to hear the rest of the story?

I answered, "Of course."

He continued. "I followed alongside that path for awhile, and I could see it was leading up to the side of a cliff. I was really afraid of being ambushed by someone, so I was very careful, took my time.

"I actually kind of circled around and came in along the cliff from another angle until I could see where the path went. It disappeared behind some rockfall up against the cliff.

"Now, there are tons of caves in this area, it's pocketed with them, like I said before, it's limestone. Spelunkers love this region, and they even found an Indian fellow inside a cave a few years ago. Archaeologists came in and recovered the body. It was very well preserved and carbon dated at around 5,000 years old."

Sam paused and sipped more coffee, then continued.

"So now I was beginning to suspect this was the entrance to a cave, and the trail had been made by cavers. I knew now it wasn't no grow op, you can't grow pot inside a cave with no electricity, so I relaxed a bit. I hid my pack in some nearby bushes.

"I sat there awhile, surveying it, until I felt comfortable going in. I quietly went down off the little hill I was on and looked in the rocks, and sure enough, there was a dark hole.

"It wasn't really big, but large enough that two or three people could enter it side by side if they wanted. But as I was looking at it, I found more of those runic things. They were carved all around the cave entrance. Carved into the rock, mind you.

"Why would someone take the time to do that? It would take forever to carve, even though it's limestone. There's a photo of the entrance, you can see it later.

"I always carry a headlamp in my pack, and I dug it out and carefully entered the hole.

"I will confess I was scared, but the wanting to know what was going on led me in there. Actually, you have no idea how scared I was, Prof. The place gave me the creeps.

"It took awhile for my eyes to adjust, so I stood there in the entrance with my headlamp off for a bit. Actually, I moved a bit to the side so I wouldn't give someone a profile to shoot at or whatever. You can never be too careful in a situation like that.

"The hole opened up into a bit of an alcove, maybe about 10 feet high by 15 wide. I stood there, checking it out.

"Could be that was all there was to it and it was someone's home or something. I have run into a few hermits, and they usually aren't very friendly. I even had one try to rob me.

"There was nobody in there, so I turned on my light and looked around.

"More runes or whatever they are, but now above another hole in the back wall. The cave went on in. I took a photo. You'll see it, Prof.

"Now things were getting dicey. The hole was easily big enough for me, but it looked like a tunnel, and I really hate being in dark narrow places. I'm a bit claustrophobic.

"I nearly bailed at that point, what business did I have being in there? But something kept me going. I have no idea what, I'm not much of an underground explorer at all.

"I slipped into the tunnel, wondering if somehow I would hear a clang as someone closed a gate behind me. I was pretty nervous. I decided I would only go in a short ways, then bail.

"I hadn't gone more than 20 feet when a bunch of bats came flying out, right in my face. OK, that scared the crap out of me, right then and there. I stopped and caught my breath and thought, what scared those bats out? Was it me, or was there something or someone back in there?

"I decided it had to be me, 'cause if there was someone in there the bats would already be gone. I could now see a bigger area ahead, and I knew my light was shining into another room, so I went ahead, but I can tell you, I had my knife ready.

"I came into the room, and this one was really big, maybe 30 by 30 feet. It seemed huge after crawling through that tunnel. And I now noticed a really overpowering dank smell, I have no idea what that was, maybe the bats.

"Once again, I stepped aside and surveyed the situation, and turned my headlamp off.

"So, Prof, I stood there listening and I finally turned on my light and surveyed the room. I had to walk around to get the full picture. There were no other holes, this appeared to be it, the end of the cave.

"As I walked around, I could see more runes carved into the walls. They seemed to kind of point to a certain place. They were in a thin line until you kind of got to this place, then they were thick. It was like a ribbon around the cave wall that culminated in a bunch of runes.

"And under that bunch of runes was a little table, made of deer antlers. It was crude, but someone had jumbled antlers together until they formed a small table. You may have seen something like it, sort of a folk art.

"And on that little table was a book. A very crude book. It was about a foot thick and maybe two feet square. Once again, there's a photo.

"I have no idea what it was made from, but the cover was leather, looked like chewed deer hide, very soft and pliable.

"I stood there for a long time, thinking about all the stories I'd heard of weirdoes doing sacrifices and all that, Druid types, you know, hippies. I was freaked out and wanted to run like hell, but something made me stay.

"I wanted more photos, and then I would get out. I needed photos so I would later know I wasn't crazy. Plus, I was curious.

"I really hesitated to touch it, but I slowly opened the book.

"It felt like it was made of some kind of homemade paper, very rough, and it smelled like that dusky odor I mentioned before—strong, almost made me gag.

"I opened it, though, and I took photos of every page. I hurried as fast as I could. I felt like I was a spy on some kind of mission.

"When I was done, I got the hell out. I actually ran down that passage and out the door and up the hill where I'd stashed my pack. I grabbed it and headed back for my truck, staying completely off that path. I just had the creepiest feeling about that place and wanted nothing more to do with it.

"Once I got back to my truck, I hauled ass out of there. I've never been back. I have no idea why I took all those photos, they kind of give me the creeps and it's not a good feeling. I kind of wish I'd never found that place."

Sam now got up and looked out my window. He seemed nervous, so I reassured him he'd done the right thing, that mysteries are best when solved, it takes the fear away.

I promised if he'd bring back the disc, I'd do my best to figure out the runes, but I also told him it's impossible to decipher anything without context. He seemed ready to leave, so I let it go at that.

I asked him one last question. "Sam, what was in the book?"

He looked puzzled, then asked, "I didn't tell you?"

"No," I replied.

"Well, dammit, they were full of the runes. And there were a couple of drawings. You'll see when I bring back the pictures. You know, Prof, that was about five months ago, and I can't get that place out of my mind. That's why I decided I needed help, to figure it all out. I want to forget it."

He was half out the door, then turned and thanked me for my time, seeming almost embarrassed. I assured him I would do my best to get to the bottom of things.

At this point, I was deeply interested and wanted him to return with the photos. I once again assured him his secret would stay with me.

We shook hands and he left. I would never believe him if I hadn't seen a few of the photos.

I barely had time to finish grading papers and get to my class, and I was completely distracted through my lecture about the history of the English language.

After I returned, Judy stopped me and asked what the visit had been about.

I just laughed and said, "Oh, some wild story about finding some strange language. If he returns, let him come up. He's very entertaining, a real character."

And I let it go at that, expecting to never see Sam again.

I went back up to my office to prepare for another class, but I couldn't concentrate. I kept seeing his photos of the runes and wondering if it was all fake, or if perhaps he hadn't discovered evidence that the Vikings had been here, or that perhaps the Native Americans did indeed have a written language. If either were true, it was the stuff linguists would die for.

The next day, Judy brought up a package for me. It was bubble wrapped and taped with my name on it. It was from

Sam. I wondered why he hadn't come up when he brought it, but the note inside answered my question:

Prof, don't need paprz, trst u, livng in pickup, leevng, wll be in tuch, do yr best, sam

I opened the package, and out fell a disc, along with photocopies of his notebook. I almost started shaking, I was so eager to see what he'd found and examine it in detail.

I put the disc in my computer, hoping it worked, which it did. I felt like a spy on a mission, just like Sam had described his feelings when he photographed the book.

I eagerly printed out each of the photos. There were over 100 total—some were of the runes around the cave entrance, some of the interior of the cave, but most were of the contents of the book.

I printed everything. I had to insert a new ink cartridge in the middle of the job, but I finally had hardcopy. I made a cup of coffee and sat down to examine everything. I had all afternoon and evening, as my next class wasn't until tomorrow.

The first photo was of Sam's truck. Why he'd photographed his truck I'll never know, but I was later very grateful that he had, because one could also make out the Colorado plates.

They were Pioneer Plates, which meant he was a descendant of original Colorado pioneers, as one had to prove their family had been in the state for 100 years to get such plates. I was surprised he'd go for the prestige. His truck was an old blue Dodge, and it had a camper on the back of similar vintage.

The next photo was of a sign. I do this myself, I often take pictures of signs to later identify where the photos were taken. I think Sam forgot that photo was on the disc, because it identified the area his cave was in, and he wanted it kept secret. But I wasn't about to tell anyone, as I had my own vested interests at this point.

The sign said "Coffeepot Springs." I suspected there would be more than one Coffeepot Springs in the state, but it was a start.

The next series of photos were of the path, which was very faint and hard to make out, but gave one an idea of what the terrain looked like. Rugged.

After that, there were a few photos of the cave entrance and then close-ups of the runes carved in the rock around the cave. Then came a few of the first room, then the tunnel, then the next big room.

Then came the gravy, so to speak. Photos of the runes carved around the big room, then of the book. It was big, and rough looking, just as he'd described it.

If he were trying to hoax me, he was doing a remarkably good job of it. Next were photos of each page, very legible.

Then I stopped, shocked. These must be the sketches he had referred to. There were two of them, dark figures that were very muscular, with broad faces and wide shoulders, and faces that looked almost human, very intelligent.

One wore a sort of crown that looked like it was made of antlers. The other looked female, it was less massive, and wore a crown made of leaves. Both were impressive looking, with heads that came to a sort of crest, or point, their shoulders melting into the neck muscles. And both were covered completely with dark hair, head to toe.

I sat back for a moment, not knowing what to think. Were these some conjured mythic figures that went with the stories in the text? Or were they sketches of real creatures?

I shivered a bit, then got up and closed the window. It was spring, and still a bit chilly.

There were more pages of runes, and now I was to the end of the photos, and there were four pictures that I couldn't figure out. They looked like photos of the ground.

I put down the photocopies and went back to the computer and enlarged the first of the four strange photos. I sat and looked at the screen, unable to make anything out.

Just then one of my students, Roger, came into my office. He looked at my screen and said, "Wow, those are really big footprints. What are they?"

Footprints? I got up and walked across the room a bit and then, there they were, footprints, clear as day. I was just too close to make out the difference between the prints and the dirt, but now it was obvious.

"I have no idea what they are, Roger, they were brought in by some guy with some other photos. Hey, stick around a minute and look at the rest, maybe you can help me figure them out."

I pulled up the other three photos onto the screen and sure enough, Roger had no trouble at all making them out, more footprints.

We studied them a bit, comparing them to nearby plants, and we deduced they were in the range of 20 inches long and about 8 inches wide. They looked like a huge barefoot human foot with wide feet and big toes.

"Bigfoot," Roger remarked. This made me stop, as his assessment fit perfectly with the sketches.

Roger was intrigued and wanted to know more, but I wasn't able to tell him, since I'd made an agreement with Sam.

But I did consider that maybe Roger would make a good partner in the project—he was very bright and knew linguistic analysis, I had taught him myself. I decided to share the story with him after talking to Sam and seeing if it were OK.

I told Roger I couldn't say anything now, but would like to include him in on it later, if I were given permission to do so.

He looked at me with a sparkle in his eyes that said he would never let a simple promise stand in the way of a good adventure, and I should just tell him now. I laughed and asked if he'd ever heard of Coffeepot Springs.

He had. Interestingly enough, Roger had grown up in the small tourist town of Glenwood Springs, Colorado, and he and his dad had hiked that area. There was a Coffeepot Springs up on the Flattop Mountains above town some ways out.

"Were there caves up there?" I asked. He said there were caves all over the Flattops, it was limestone.

This was too easy, I now knew the probable area of the cave. But there was a lot of territory up there, one could look forever, I realized.

Roger sat there, puzzled and with a look on his face that asked to be let in on this one. And I wanted him in on it, I knew he could help me figure out if this was some kind of language.

He was a bright and hard-working graduate student, and I was an overworked professor trying to get tenure. But I had given Sam my word.

Fast forward a few weeks. I'd been working in my spare time trying to figure out what the runic mystery was all about. I'd copied them into a notebook, studied their sequences and patterns, and done all a trained linguist can do to analyze a language.

But I was getting nowhere, because one needs a framework, a context, for figuring out a foreign language or system. That's why the Rosetta Stone is so famous, it provided the link between the old and the new. I needed a Rosetta Stone.

I had determined that the inscriptions were probably made by different writers, as there were differences and similarities. They also looked like the real deal, not a hoax.

I needed more information before I could even guess at when they were made. I needed to see them up close on the stone to determine how old they were using dating methods. My archaeologist friends needed to be there with me. And I needed that book.

I also needed more information from Sam, but he had left no way to contact him, no phone, no address, nothing. I also wanted his permission to get Roger involved. Until he returned, I was pretty much at a dead end.

Then, one day in early May, after I'd pretty much given up, Sam showed up in my office. He looked exactly the same, down to the clothes and boots and haircut, or lack of one. I made him a cup of coffee.

"Hey, Prof, havin' any luck?"

I told him what I'd been able to find out, and what I needed—to see the inscriptions for myself with an expert archaeologist. I also needed some kind of intermediary translation, which I doubted would be forthcoming.

I had compared his runes with those of the Norse and they had absolutely nothing in common. I was now thinking it was a completely independent system and probably Native American, but I wanted to show them to a runic expert.

I was frustrated, I needed more information, I needed help, and I needed to know where these things were located.

But Sam wouldn't tell me anything more. He could see how earnest I was at solving the mystery, but he didn't trust me enough to show me where to go.

I added, "And Sam, my friend, I need to be able to get in touch with you occasionally. Not being able to reach you has slowed this thing down, you know."

Sam nodded, then said there was no way because he lived in his truck and had no phone. He assured me he would check in whenever he could.

The only thing I could think of doing at this point was to send Sam back and have him collect the data we needed, since he wouldn't reveal the location.

I could get him in touch with an archaeologist who could walk him through how to measure the depth of the carved inscriptions, bring back rock samples, more detailed photos, that kind of thing.

Sam said that would be OK, as long as no one else was let in on what was going on. I agreed to keep the secret from all but Roger, who would also be sworn to secrecy.

I called Roger and he came up to my office. Sam OK'd Roger's help, after meeting him to gauge his trustworthiness. I don't think Roger had any idea what he'd gotten himself into, because when we explained it all, he looked as incredulous as I had—and excited.

I told Sam he could park his rig in my driveway, which he did, but he wouldn't come inside. I did manage to sneak a photo of him from inside the house. I don't know why, but I just wanted some sort of verification this guy really did exist and wasn't a product of my imagination. I was later glad I did, though at the time it felt sneaky.

The three of us spent part of the next day meeting with an archaeology prof and getting the information we needed to try and date the inscriptions. I also went down and bought a better camera for Sam to try and get more photos.

Sam was very quiet through all of this, and when it came time for him to leave the next morning, I flat out asked him if the location wasn't in the Flattops. He didn't seem surprised and noted that I must've seen the sign for Coffeepot Springs. I said I had.

He then said, and I'll never forget it, "This isn't at all what you think it is, Prof, it isn't Indians."

I asked him what it was.

"Didn't you see the footprints? That should tell you. Those footprint photos were taken right outside the cave. I don't want to go back. I don't care about what it is anymore. It's too dangerous."

He handed me the camera I'd given him. "Thanks, but I just can't do this."

"Sam, can you tell me where it is so I can go in there?" I asked.

"No, it's too dangerous. I'm wishing I'd never told anybody about this."

"What is it, Sam, if it's not Indians? Tell me."

He paused, then said, "Bigfoot. It's some kind of a Bigfoot holy place, or their history, or something. Nobody belongs in there, I know that."

I was a bit shocked, but I remembered that Roger had said the same thing, Bigfoot. I then told Sam I'd spent many hours on this and it was definitely a real language, it had the pattern frequencies, the markings of consonants and vowels, and I'd even been able to make out some of the syntax. I wasn't ready to quit.

But now I realized that I should've quit right then and there. Maybe Sam would still be alive, assuming he's dead.

But I didn't quit. I was able to talk Sam into going back, against his better judgement, and I suspect that he may have lost his life because of that. He listened to me instead of his own instincts.

Anyway, Sam went back out, promising more photos and the information we needed to try and date the inscriptions. He would also try to get a sample of the paper without harming the book. There was no way he would even consider bringing the book back.

I gave him a cell phone, and he promised to use it to call me in a week or so when he got back from the cave so I'd know he was OK.

A week went by, and I began anticipating Sam's call. Nothing. Two weeks, nothing.

In the meantime, Roger was now working on the runes, trying to see what he could come up with.

At the beginning of the third week, we agreed we needed to notify officials of Sam's absence. I called the sheriff in Garfield County and emailed them the photo of Sam's truck, along with the photo of him I'd taken, and I mentioned Coffeepot Springs.

They sent out a search party that same day. They found his truck, sitting at the springs, but no Sam.

Two days later, I received another call from search and rescue. They hadn't found him, and they were going to give up the search, as a big spring storm was in the area. It was snowing, and they were dealing with whiteout conditions. They would try to get back in there when the storm lifted.

But they had found tracks about two miles from the springs, going up against a mountainside. There was enough fresh snow that they'd managed to track him.

They were worried he'd run into a bear, as there were lots of big footprints around his in the snow, but melted and not very clear. But the bears should still be in hibernation, so they weren't sure what was going on.

I asked if they'd found a camera or cell phone, and they had found a camera in his pickup, but no phone. But there was no coverage up there, anyway. They said they would send me the camera.

I felt sick. I was responsible for this, he hadn't wanted to go back and I'd talked him into it. Roger said it was ultimately Sam's decision, his choice, no matter what I'd said to him, and I shouldn't feel guilty—but I did anyway.

I put the runes on the top shelf, so to speak, and halted the project. I was tempted to throw everything away, now that Sam was missing and maybe even dead. I received the camera, but I didn't even want to look at its contents, so I gave it to Chris.

I still had no idea where the cave was, except in a general sense, although I thought it might be located using the information on the first page of Sam's notebook. I was torn between wanting to go find the cave and hopefully Sam also, or forgetting it ever existed.

Could Sam have had a run-in with Bigfoot? I had no idea such creatures might really exist, I thought it was just a legend from the Pacific Northwest. But in Colorado? Bigfoot? The mystery haunted me, and I couldn't forget it, but I also now wanted nothing to do with it.

After two weeks of looking, search and rescue gave up the hunt. Sam would stay missing until he either came in by himself or someone found his body. I hoped for the former. I suspected it would be the latter.

Then, one day in mid-June, Roger walked into my office. He was excited.

"Professor Johnson, I've found it! I think we can solve the rune mystery!"

I was shocked.

He continued, "You know, I'm doing some work on the Lakota Archive with Professor Taylor. I came upon something really weird in an old manuscript from the museum in Bismarck, North Dakota. It was a photocopy of an old sun calendar they have in their archives with some Siouan inscriptions they thought we might be interested in."

He pulled out the copy and pointed to an inscription in one corner. "Look, Professor. Runes. And under them, Lakota Sioux. It looks like a translation. There's a lot of them. If it is, it may be enough to break them."

I was dumbfounded. Were the Lakota Sioux ever in the Flattops area, or were there Bigfoot in other regions? Had these huge creatures, if they even existed, actually communicated with the Native Americans?

Was Sam right, was the cave some kind of archive for them? Had they killed Sam for entering it? It all seemed like something out of a fantasy novel.

But Roger had more. He had downloaded the photos from the camera I had given Sam, and there were photos that looked to be a new cave. There, on its wall, were more runes, and under them, more Lakota Sioux.

I was astounded.

To make a long story short, as they say, Roger and I are working on the runes, and we think we may indeed have the key. We are now trying to translate the book, and are having some success, although there are some gaps. What we're finding is amazing, to put it mildly. It seems to be a historical account.

I am currently grappling with the ethical considerations of revealing this information to others. It's a fascinating manuscript, but do I have the right to print it? I don't know. It's a real issue for me, and one I may never be able to answer.

On one hand, this is very sensitive information about a creature not even believed by most to exist. And on the other, it would solve many mysteries and perhaps provide more evidence for their existence and ultimately, their protection.

But my reputation as a credible professor of linguistics could also be at stake if I were to publish the information.

I keep hoping Sam will walk in the door. If and when he does, I suspect there will be more solutions to this mystery.

Until then, Roger and I will keep working on this amazing project.

About the Author

· ·

Rusty Wilson grew up in the state of Washington, in the heart of Bigfoot country. He didn't know a thing about Bigfoot until he got lost at the age of six and was then found and subsequently adopted by a kindly Bigfoot family.

He lived with them until he was 16, when they finally gave up on ever socializing him into Bigfoot ways (he hated garlic and pancakes, refused to sleep in a nest, wouldn't hunt wild pigs, and on top of it all, his feet were small).

His Bigfoot family then sent him off to Evergreen State College in nearby Olympia, thinking it would be liberal enough to take care of a kid with few redeeming qualities, plus they liked the thick foliage around the college and figured Rusty could live there, saving them money for housing.

At Evergreen, Rusty studied wildlife biology, eventually returning to the wilds, after first learning to read and write and regale everyone with his wild tales. He eventually became a flyfishing guide, and during his many travels in the wilds, he collected stories from others who have had contact with Bigfoot, also known as Sasquatch.

Because of his background, Rusty is considered to be the world's foremost Bigfoot expert (at least so by himself, if not by anyone else). He's spent many a fun evening around campfires with his clients, telling stories. Some of those clients had some pretty good stories of their own. And now, for the first time, he's willing to share their stories with you. He's also working on a book about his own experiences.

Whether you're a Bigfoot believer or not, we hope you enjoyed these tall tales...or are they really true stories?

Only Rusty and his fellow story tellers know for sure.

If you enjoyed this book, you will also like *Rusty Wilson's More Bigfoot Campfire Stories*, the second in this series.

Also check out *The Ghost Rock Cafe* by Chinle Miller, a Bigfoot mystery. All are available at yellowcatbooks.com, Barnes and Noble, and Amazon.com.

MAR   2013

Made in the USA
Lexington, KY
04 March 2013